I0788543

Fishing & Forgery

A Paranormal Witch Cozy Mystery

Book Store Cozy Mystery Series
Book 11

Lucinda Race

MC Two Press

Editor NN Light Editing Services
Cover design by Mariah Sinclair

Manufactured in the United States of America
First Edition April 2025

Print Edition ISBN 978-1-966424-10-9
Large Print 978-1-966-424-18-5

Hardcover 978-1-966-424-19-2
E-book ISBN 978-1-954520-98-1

1. Robin's Cafe
2. Bygone Antiques
3. The Pembroke Cliffs
4. Cozy Nook Bookstore
5. Twisted Scissors Hair Salon
6. Betty's Market
7. Old Town Library
8. Miss Judy's Dance Studio
9. The Sweet Spot Baker
10. Bee Bee's Boutique
11. Tuckers Hardware Store
12. The Copper Kettle
13. Police Station
14. Town Hall

Chapter 1
Lily

QUICK NOTE: If you enjoy Fishing & Forgery, check out my offer for a FREE novella at the end. With that, happy reading.

* * *

I leaned against the vinyl boat cushion and tipped my face to the sun. "I can't believe the wedding is a little over a month away."

From the captain's seat, Gage laughed. "And we've gone fishing."

The boat trolled along at a sedate pace. Nikki and Steve were setting up fishing poles, Sharon and EL were sitting on the bow with their heads together, chatting, and Mac and his wife Margaret were talking quietly. I sighed. This was a perfect way to unwind from wedding preparations and work, which was an issue for tomorrow.

Milo, my sweet gray kitty, waddled across the deck and clumsily jumped up beside me. "My dear witch, I'm not a fan of this life jacket. I can barely move, and it's bright orange." He shuddered. "Talk about a fashion faux pas."

I scratched under his chin and, speaking softly, said, "My dear familiar. Should I remind you that you're not a fan of water, and we're two hundred yards offshore? That's a long way to swim should you fall overboard."

With a grumble, he said, "I'd have to swim if the sharks didn't get me first." Snapping his head in my direction, he glared at me. "Wait. You wouldn't jump in and save me?"

I laughed. "Of course I would. I'd go to the ends of the earth to protect you, which is why you're wearing that ugly orange life vest."

Milo sniffed. "I wouldn't call it ugly, and I wear it well." He looked at the lovebirds on the boat's bow. "I'm happy that Sharon and EL are dating. They deserve someone special in their lives."

Grinning, I said, "Look at you being all romantic. Is there someone special for you?"

He groaned, "This familiar only loves two things in life—any fish, hence that's why I'm on a boat in the middle of the Atlantic Oceanand my witch."

I smothered a laugh. "We're hardly in the middle of the ocean."

"It feels like it," he grumbled before he did his best attempt at stretching out across the seat as the boat broke through the small waves.

Margaret crossed the deck and sat down

next to Milo. "It's sweet that you brought your kitty fishing with us today. We talked about bringing the baby, but I think the sun would be too hot for her."

"Milo loves to be wherever I am, and I'm pretty sure he thinks he's supervising. Cat, fish, dinner, and I understand that there's too much sun for Amanda. Maybe next time will be better."

"What do you think we'll catch today? This is my first time fishing."

"Not even on a lake or river?" I was surprised since Mac was an enthusiastic fisherman, but I believed couples didn't have to be enamored with everything their partner did to be happy.

She shook her head. "I know what you must be thinking. Mac loves everything to do with fish, from eating to catching. But there's always been something to do, and I couldn't make it."

"Life keeps us busy." I looked at Gage and thought of the close call we had several weeks ago when he was kidnapped. Once we returned to a new normal, we had a long talk. We'd make it a point to have more fun with our friends and family. "You have to make time for what's important."

Margaret placed her hand over mine. "You must still be dealing with the ripple effects from what happened."

I appreciated that she didn't say kidnap. It was like a cold dagger driven into my soul. "We're focusing on the wedding and the festivities leading up to it, like this excursion."

"I wanted to thank you for inviting us." She looked at Mac and then at me. "My husband thinks the world of you and Gage."

"That's sweet of you to say. We're happy we've become friends, too."

She bent close. "Do you think I actually need to hold a pole to make it official?"

"To be a friend or a fisherwoman?" I winked. "The first, you already are, and the second, if you want to fish, then go for it; otherwise, stretch out on a bench and relax. You can always hang out with Milo. There's plenty of food and drinks in the coolers; help yourself."

I rose to my feet. "Gage, is it time to drop anchor?"

He cut the power and nodded. "Go for it." The boat bobbed gently on the swells. The anchor slipped with a splash into the briny depths. "Steve, are we ready to cast a line?"

"I am, even if you're not." Steve adjusted his ball cap and held out a pole to me. "Lily, ready?"

I took it and with a flick of my wrist, the hook and line slipped under the water's surface before I settled back on the bench. I never catch anything, and I didn't expect today to be any different. "Margaret, join me. This is the most fun you'll have fishing." I gave her a wink and patted the space next to me.

"I'm not sure I know how?" Her voice went up at the end of the sentence, and she glanced around. "I don't want to look foolish."

Mac was baiting a hook and handed his wife the pole. "If you get a tug, let me know, and I'll help you reel it in." He kissed her cheek. "Beginner's luck is always the best kind."

Gage leaned against the side. "A nice striped bass dinner on Margaret tonight is the goal."

"Don't bet on that. Instead, we'd better pick up a couple of pizzas on the way to Lily's." She held the pole with a two-handed vise grip.

Mac sat down next to her. "Honey, we're here to have fun."

She relaxed her grip and looked at me with a gritted smile. "Are you sure this is relaxing?"

I handed Gage my pole and hip-checked Mac off the seat. "My secret," I said, dropping my voice, "my hook isn't baited."

Her eyes widened, and she gave Mac a side glance. "He had a gigantic piece of something on the hook before giving me his pole."

"Do you want to switch? You'll be in the action without stressing about reeling in anything."

She nodded. I jumped up, took my pole, and handed it to her. "Sit over here."

Once we had exchanged fishing poles, I settled back on the seat. The line drifted before I tipped the pole back a bit and let the hook settle below the surface.

"How deep's the water here?" I asked no one in particular but hoped someone would answer.

"It's still shallow. If we went out a little farther, it would drop off sharply," Steve said. "Don't worry, there's good fishing here."

That's what I feared since now I had a baited line. Gage dug a bottle of water from the cooler and took the top off before handing it to me. "Here you go." As I reached for it my line started running away from the boat, jerking me in the process.

"I've got something." I tightened my grip on the pole. It bowed to the water's surface. "Uh, Gage. A hand here."

He put a steady hand on my arm. "You've

got this. Nice and easy now. Let the fish get tired. He can run for a bit."

"Why do you think it's a he?" I didn't take my eyes off the pole and continued to work the fish. It was a game of cat and mouse.

Milo settled next to me. "Oh goody, fish for supper. I hope it's huge."

Nikki smothered a grin since she was the only other person on the boat who could understand him. It was a witch thing. My shoulders tired quickly as the fish and I battled. "How long is this going to take?"

Steve was holding an oversized net and a gaff hook. "Don't worry, Lily, I'm ready."

Milo whispered, "Use magic."

I gave him a sharp look. "Absolutely not."

Margaret shrieked. "I've hooked a fish." She flashed a panicked expression in my direction. "How's that possible?"

My familiar perked up, "With no bait, it must be magic." Not that anyone but me and Nikki could understand him.

Mac perched behind her, he said, "Just like

Lily's doing, play with your fish, tire him, or her, letting the line run out, and we'll get him on the boat in no time."

"Lily's been working that one forever."

He chuckled. "It just seems that way. You've got this, Mar, and I'll help if you need it."

Now, Margaret and I were battling beasts of the ocean. I would wind up the line and then let him run. I swear the fish was getting more line than I was cranking back in to the spinning reel.

Gage said, "You're doing great."

"Do you want to take over?" I didn't dare look away; I was afraid if I loosened my grip on the pole, I'd go overboard.

"You can do this." His encouraging words made me more determined than ever to bring this fish aboard. "Maybe it's dinner."

Milo grumbled, "Doubtful, since you can't pull smoked salmon from the ocean—only our refrigerator."

A moment ago he was calling it dinner but

now was another story. I knew he was teasing me, trying to lighten my mood, but I didn't respond with a snappy retort. Staying focused was the key to success, especially in this instance.

"Margaret, how are you doing?"

"Great."

I stole a glance her way, and she grinned from ear to ear.

"I've almost got it. Every so often, I can see the brown just under the water's surface."

Brown? My line jerked. I didn't have time to think about the color of her fish. I was a little miffed that my stupid fish was so hard to reel in, like give in already.

Nikki said, "I'll get Margaret's fish. Steve, you stay with Lily."

By this time, Sharon and EL were on the stern. The energy was electric as I continued to battle what I was now referring to as dinner. My line jerked hard again. I tumbled forward. Gage grabbed the straps on my life jacket and hung on.

"Don't let go." My voice wobbled as the line tightened and then whipped forward again. This time, I fell back against Gage. The line came sailing through the air and landed in the boat, but it was missing the hook...and more importantly, the fish.

Scrambling to my feet, I ran the line through my hand until I looked at the end. "What the heck? I've been robbed! No fish and no hook, either."

"And there goes dinner," Milo grumbled and flopped on the cushion.

I couldn't respond to him without looking foolish, which wasn't helping my annoyance. I focused my attention on Margaret, who seemed to enjoy the experience of reeling in her big one.

"I might just be providing dinner after all." She shot a grin in my direction, and her enthusiasm was contagious. Everyone in the group gave her helpful tips as her fish grew closer to the boat.

She leaned to the side. "Hey, look, I'm

bringing up seaweed." Cranking the spinner even more, it was apparent the catch of the day was growing closer with each turn of the reel.

Steve leaned over the edge of the boat with the net.

Nikki held onto his belt even as he drew closer to the water.

"Be careful."

As I composed the impromptu spell, he said, "Got it."

Steve pulled the line closer to the boat. "What do we have here?"

Margaret clutched the pole. "Is it huge?"

He tossed the clumps of seaweed back into the water and hauled it up. Weighing down the net was an oversized brown leather satchel. Water poured from the seams when Steve set it on the boat. "Great catch, but this won't be dinner."

Sharon said, "This reminds me of pirate treasure. We should look inside and see if we can discover who this belongs to. I'm sure the owner will be grateful to have it back."

Nikki laughed. "No pirate treasure for us. We went down that path for our wedding." She gave a mock shudder. "I'd love to see what's inside, though."

Gage knelt next to the bag. He examined the clasp. "It looks in good shape. I'd guess it hasn't been in the water long. Maybe we'll find something to identify the owner and, like Sharon said, return it."

Milo slunk forward. "And maybe there's a reward that will buy me some smoked salmon."

I picked him up. "You need to stay out of the way. We don't know for sure what's inside. Maybe it's something that can harm a cute little cat such as yourself."

"My dear witch, thank you for putting me first before your curiosity." He purred, and I scratched the top of his head.

One-way conversations with Milo were always interesting.

"Sharon, on the off chance we need proof of the finding, would you take pictures?"

"Gage, you can't be serious. It's a simple

bag we pulled from the ocean. You shouldn't always try to connect it with a crime."

The group chuckled since I had an interesting habit of getting involved in many cases Gage and the Pembroke Cove Police Department had worked on over the years.

Withdrawing her cell, Sharon said, "Ready when you are, boss." Some habits were hard to break; she still referred to Gage as boss or detective even when they weren't at work. At least boss was less formal.

He pushed on the catch and tugged on the sides, but it wouldn't give way. He repeated the procedure two more times without success. "EL, under the captain's seat there's a small toolbox. In there I have a Swiss army knife. Grab it for me?"

Excitement rippled through the group.

I asked, "Gage, what do you think is inside?"

He gave me a quick glance and laughed. "Someone's underwear and socks."

EL handed him the knife. A moment later,

the blade popped the latch, opening the bag. I tried to peer in, but Gage was in the way.

"What do you see?"

He gave a low whistle. "Definitely not socks." His gaze circled the group. "Sweetheart, friends, and fellow detectives, we have a bag full of money."

Chapter 2
Lily

"How much money? Do you think someone robbed a bank, or maybe it's their life savings?" My annoyance at not catching a fish evaporated. "EL, grab my tote bag. Inside the pocket are latex gloves."

He arched a brow. "You carry gloves with you?"

I lifted a shoulder. "My new motto is you can never be too prepared."

He did as I asked and handed a pair to Gage.

Sharon was still taking pictures from all angles as we crowded around Gage and the bag. Everyone had forgotten about fishing.

"How much cash do you think is in there?"

Gage looked at me. "I'm not taking it out of the bag here. We'll do that back at the station."

"Great. I'll get the anchor. Mac, the satchel will fit in a large bag at the bottom of my tote. We can seal it for evidence."

Sharon looked up, her brow wrinkled. "It's like you've got a Mary Poppins bag."

Nikki said, "You have no idea."

Gage scanned the group. "Is everyone ready to call it a day? I want to get back to the station and see what we can find out about the money. I haven't heard of any bank robberies recently."

Mac, Sharon, and EL shook their heads.

I looked at Nikki, who shrugged her shoulders. "Finding a bag full of money is better than finding a dead body."

I groaned. "Now you've jinxed us." My laugh had a nervous edge as I looked across the

water, hoping that we wouldn't find a body bobbing. That would be just too much reality on
what was supposed to be a carefree day.

Mac secured the bag, Sharon took a few
more pictures, and Margaret, Steve, and Nikki
sat down and prepared for the return trip back
to the dock.

I sat in the seat next to Gage and held Milo
in my lap. "Any theories yet?"

"No, you?"

"We need more facts before I spin out
ideas." I watched as our small marina came into
view. "You know this is one of two things. Either someone is frantic because they lost a boat-
load of money, or the money's stolen and two
someones are frantic. The original person and
the thief."

Gage dropped the boat speed with a
solemn nod as we entered the no-wake zone
leading into our slip. He gave me a shoulder
bump. "I'm sorry we cut our fishing trip short,
but we should get right on this."

"I agree. We'll still have a barbeque together, so when you're done at the station, everyone should come back to the house."

He leaned over and kissed me lightly on the lips. "You're terrific."

I perked up. "So are you."

As we slid next to the dock, Steve jumped out and tied the stern and bow lines, and then he added the spring line for good measure. "All secured, Gage." He held his hand out for Sharon, Margaret, Nikki, and myself. Then, he waited for the guys to disembark before EL and Steve grabbed the coolers.

Mac had the evidence bag and moved at a rapid pace to Gage's vintage cherry red pickup truck.

"I'm going to stow this in the bed."

Sharon and EL were on motorcycles, Mac and Margaret were driving his dune buggy, and Nikki and Steve weren't police officers, so they couldn't transport the bag.

Nikki waved. "See you at your place later?"

"I'll call you with the plan." I got into the

passenger seat, Milo was in my lap, and Gage said, "You're coming with me?"

"Of course. This is too interesting to wait and get a second-hand update." I waved at the road in front of us. "Drive, Detective Cutie."

Milo said, "Hey, that's my line."

I ran my hand down the length of his back, and he purred. "Well, you can call him that, too."

Gage started the truck. "Do I need to remind you this is a police matter?"

"Of course not. Besides, I think my forte is murder, not found money." I looked out the side window and wondered where the mystery of the satchel would lead. My gut was telling me this wasn't an accidental loss of a piece of luggage.

The trip to the station didn't take long. I carried Milo up the steps to the back entrance. Gage punched in the security code and he held the door for me. Sharon and EL zipped into the parking lot and ran up the steps behind us.

Sharon said, "Mac is dropping Margaret at

their place and he'll be along." The heavy steel door closed with a thud. The cement and linoleum floor swallowed the slap of her deck shoes.

Concentrating on Sharon kept me from allowing the thrill of a new mystery to carry me away or, as I liked to call them, puzzles.

EL fell into step next to me as Gage and Sharon led the way. His voice was low as he said, "It's written on your face."

Giving him a quizzical glance, I said, "I'm not sure what you're talking about." Of course, I knew, but I wasn't about to reveal it.

"The twist of your mouth, the way your eyes are sparkling. The bag of money has your brain in overdrive."

I schooled myself to provide a more neutral look. "Don't you think it's curious? Bringing up a bag from the ocean? Who knows how it got there and who it belongs to. It's interesting."

"Remember, I'm a different part of this investigative equation. I'm a lab rat." He held open the next door, and we stepped into the heart of the station. Officers Shepard and Jonesy were talking, and Alice—the front desk clerk—was filling her water bottle.

She looked at our little group and asked, "Aren't you supposed to be fishing?"

Gage held up the clear garbage bag. "Margaret caught a fresh case for us. This satchel is full of money."

Jessie Shepard gave a low whistle. "Now that's what I call a catch of the day." He slapped me a high five.

Jonesy said, "Detective, life isn't dull with Lily around."

He gave me a wink. "You have no idea." Holding the bag up, he bobbed his head toward the door. "We'll be in the conference room."

Sharon said, "I'll get my laptop."

Milo squirmed. "Should I hang around or head for home?"

I kept my voice low. "Stay. This might be fun."

"Only you would enjoy fishing for a police case instead of dinner."

For his ears alone, I said, "We'll have fish for dinner. I'll text Nikki and ask her to run down to the marina and pick up striper."

"I want my own fish," he grumbled.

Setting Milo on a chair, I pulled out my cell, sent Nikki a quick message, and was ready to take as many pictures as possible before Gage noticed. We both knew I'd get the details one way or the other, but this was part of the fun for me, trying to outwit my handsome fiancé.

Sharon rolled out a sheet of white paper to cover the tabletop. It made me think of paper used to wrap fish. "Why are you putting this paper out?"

EL said, "To maintain any evidence that could be small and get lost on the actual table. We'll fold it up and put it in a new evidence bag, just to be certain. Sometimes, I've tested particles and residue from an object and found important clues."

I nodded. "Huh, I never knew that. Learn something new every day."

Gage pulled on a fresh pair of latex gloves, and Sharon did the same. Just as they opened the bag, Mac strode in.

"Sorry, I checked on Amanda when I dropped Margaret off."

"No problem, we're just getting started." Gage eased open the bag and extracted the leather tote. He had snapped it shut while still on the boat. This was almost as exciting as the first time.

I stepped closer, my cell at the ready.

"Wait," Sharon said, "Let me get the evidence camera. Better resolution."

Dang it, I was hoping to keep this rolling along before Gage noticed my phone. I tucked it behind my back.

He caught me trying to appear aloof. "Lily, I won't stop you from taking pictures."

"You won't?"

"Nope, for once, it's straightforward, a lost bag, but we're going to treat it as it was more. Just to err on the side of caution."

His words didn't deflate my excitement.

Sharon came back and held up the camera. "Ready when you are, boss."

The five of us and Milo crowded around the table. Gage opened the bag wider and withdrew the water-logged satchel. He carefully set the plastic bag aside. I took a picture of the clear bag, the droplets of water, and bits of ocean before focusing on the open satchel. He pulled out bundles of money in clear Ziploc bags secured with purple zippers; inside were stacks of cash three to four inches tall, each wrapped with what I thought was a ponytail holder. A bank would use paper.

My heart rate ticked up as the excitement became palpable in the room.

Mac and Sharon exchanged a questioning look. Gage pulled stack after stack out and at the bottom he held up a knife with a wood handle that I guessed had a seven-inch blade and a 9mm Glock handgun. I was familiar with the gun, since it was like what Gage carried for work. He checked to make sure the safety was on before placing it on the table next to the blade. Relief replaced the shudder of fear racing down my spine. The gun could have gone off in the truck.

"This just got interesting." I was hitting the shutter button as fast as I could from different angles, including the knife and gun.

EL said, "I'll need to test the bills and check the serial numbers on the money and gun against reports of stolen firearms, if there are any."

"Do you think it's counterfeit?" It was the question on everyone's mind. Even if no one said it, I would.

"It's possible." Gage placed each stack in a row.

Milo said, "Do we have a case?"

I echoed his question to Gage.

"If this is counterfeit, we'll turn it over to the feds. That's out of our jurisdiction."

"And if it's stolen, is that within yours?"

He stepped back from the table. "Potentially. Sharon, finish up and we'll put this in an official evidence bag. EL, can you look into this tomorrow?"

"I can start today if you'd like." He gave Sharon an apologetic look.

"No, it's Sunday. We're going to take the rest of the day off. Once we wrap this up, we'll head over to Lily's, crank up the grill, and turn on some tunes."

I grinned. "Remember, we're blowing off steam before the wedding craziness is upon us. Can we chalk this up to a minor detour of the day and get back to having fun?"

Gage said, "You heard the lady." He tossed me the keys to his truck. "Why don't you head back to the house and get things ready? We'll be right behind you. Logging all of this won't take long."

Milo jumped to the floor. "That's the best news I've heard all day." He strutted to the closed door and waited for me to follow him.

I blew Gage a kiss. "Don't be long. Mac, when you pick up Margaret, bring Amanda, too."

"Thanks, Lily." He said, "She loves being around all the pets."

With a grumble, Milo said, "Who's he calling a pet? The only four-legged bag of bones that qualifies is Brutus."

I ignored his chatter and picked him up. "Gage, do I need to come back and get you?"

"No, I'll ride with Mac." He waved me out the door, and I got the impression there was something the official police officers wanted to discuss without me around.

I stepped out of the conference room and scratched under Milo's chin. "You need to behave when we're with a group of people that don't know you can talk or understand every word they say."

"We need to develop some kind of sign language for you to answer me. I don't like not having anyone to talk to."

I hissed, "Should I leave you home next time?" I waved to Alice as I crossed the lobby. "See you later."

"Enjoy the rest of your day, Lily."

The door closed with a *swish* behind me, and I paused on the top step. The glare of the late morning sun was blinding. I adjusted my wide-brimmed hat and slipped my dark glasses in place. It was then I noticed a person crumpled on the sidewalk, motionless. Dropping Milo to the step, I raced to the man. The side of his head was bloody and his eyes were open and unfocused. My breath caught as I pressed my fingertips to the base of his ear, hoping to feel the gentle throb of a pulse. I rocked back on my heels, scanning the area. A trail of blood came from the street and ended where he had fallen.

"Dang it, Gage won't be happy with this news." I pulled out my cell and dialed.

"Hi, Lily. Did you forget something?" His voice was soothing as my heart hammered in my chest.

My exhale was a *whoosh.* "I need you outside and tell Sharon to bring her evidence kit."

"Lily. What's happened?"

"I didn't find a dead body; one found me." I

looked at the mystery man in front of me. "Before you ask, I've never seen him before."

"We'll be right there."

I disconnected and, of course, I began snapping pictures of the man and the blood droplets from the street, and had the phone back in my pocket by the time the door to the station burst open. Gage raced down the steps.

Sharon, Mac, and EL were right behind him.

He looked at the victim and then me. "Tell me everything."

The team snapped on gloves for the second time in less than thirty minutes.

EL said, "Does anyone see a murder weapon?"

Milo meowed at EL, who knelt next to my familiar. He picked Milo up and handed him to me. "We should preserve the crime scene."

"Lily, tell him to look under the bush over there. I saw a large rock with blood on it. I bet that's the murder weapon, and they tossed it there when they dumped the body."

"EL, what's over there?" I pointed toward where Milo had said the rock was.

He and Gage crossed the grassy stretch and knelt on the ground. "It's a rock that appears to have blood on it. We need to bag it and test the blood to see if it matches the victim."

Mac flicked him an evidence bag.

EL said, "It looks fresh."

I stuck my hands in my pockets. "Well, this day took an unexpected turn. Money and a body. I wonder what'll happen next."

Chapter 3
Gage

Lily and Milo were far enough away when EL and I extracted what I suspected would be the murder weapon. "Notice something interesting about this rock?"

EL nodded. "Algae. Like something you might find near a jetty?"

"You got that right. Seems like an interesting coincidence that we find a bag full of money in the ocean and now a dead body."

"It might be too soon to link the two, but it lends itself to that conclusion. When I examine the body, I'll test the rock to see if there's any connection to particulates on the bag.

"Can we get fingerprints from the satchel?" I glanced at the dead man. "I know it's a long shot, but I wanted to put it out there."

"The areas that were exposed to salt water, definitely not, but the money in the plastic bags has potential. That should yield prints if its stolen; if it's counterfeit, then whoever produced the bills would have worn gloves to protect the ink from smudges. I'll do my best."

I clapped my hand on his shoulder. "I know you will." I peeled off my glove and stashed it in my shorts pocket. I couldn't afford to cross contaminate the scene of the crime with any fibers from EL. The sounds of a siren were growing closer. "The ambulance will be here soon."

"I'm going to the morgue and get things settled. I'll wait until tomorrow to do the full autopsy, but I'll get his prints, so at least the database can be working."

"Do you think it is possible to have any results by the end of the day tomorrow?"

EL said, "Depending on how complex it becomes, my guess is by noon I'll have something to give you. I'll look at the money first. I know it's out of my purview as the coroner. But remember I went to that seminar and there was an extensive session on the new counterfeiters of the twenty-first century. It won't take me long to apply what I learned and then we can turn it over to the Secret Service if necessary. That will give me time to either link or rule out a connection between the money and our victim."

I nodded. "EL, what do you think is the likelihood they're connected?"

He followed my gaze, "Ninety out of one hundred in favor."

I agreed with him.

Sharon approached us. "Boss, we're done taking pictures for the moment. We've bagged his hands. If he struggled with whoever attacked him, there'll be evidence. From first glance, the blow to his head is farther back on the side, but based on the blood trail down his face, the weapon connected with his temple. He might have been struck twice. Not stepping on EL's toes," she gave him a professional nod, "my conclusion is he died soon after he was struck. Based on the blood spatter leading back to the street, someone must have dropped him off and sped away. We'll need to watch the security footage."

"Okay, get Officer Shepard to review the video."

Her lips tipped down. "Gage, I was going to do that."

"I appreciate your dedication. You need a day off. We've worked hard with the investigation into the death of Madeline Swanson and other incidents. We all need a break." I wasn't about to make this personal, but I wanted to concentrate on something happy for a change, at least for an afternoon.

She opened her mouth, glanced at EL, and said, "You're right. Shepard can do the preliminary work. Mr. Doe and the satchel aren't going anywhere."

The ambulance backed over the sidewalk, effectively blocking one lane of traffic. The EMTs removed the gurney but didn't bother bringing the life-saving gear. Suzi, a veteran in the department, gave us a brisk nod.

"Detectives, Doctor." She gestured to the other woman with her. "This is Beth. She's new."

"Hello." She unbuckled the gurney straps and let them hang over the sides. "He's not having a good day."

Suzi gestured for me to follow her away from everyone. She nodded in the EMT's direction. "Beth's solid, but she has zero filter with her comments. She says it like she sees it. I hope she won't put you off."

"Does she know how to do the job?"

Suzi nodded. "Her skills are impeccable, and she was at the top of her class and internship."

"That's what I care about. Thanks for giving me a heads up. I can fill everyone in."

We returned to where Beth was waiting. She said, "Suzi filled you in about me?"

"She said you were direct. I can appreciate that approach. You won't have any problem with us." I hoped that reassured her that she'd get a fair shake. "All I expect is the best job you can do."

"Then let's get this body off the sidewalk before we draw a bunch of lookie-loos. I take it we're skipping the hospital?"

EL said, "Yes. I'll follow you to the morgue."

I stepped back to let Suzi and Beth do their job.

Mac was ready to take pictures once the body was off the sidewalk. Lily watched every move from a discreet distance, but her sunglasses couldn't disguise her interest as she leaned forward, catching every word. Milo was content in her arms, chattering.

I wondered what he had observed, and I'd ask Lily when I got the chance and when we wouldn't be overheard. Me asking about a cat's impression of the crime scene would be impossible to explain.

She lowered her glasses and then slid them back into place. I strode over to her. "What do you think?"

"There's someone inside the square, just behind the forsythia bushes, watching every move. You need to send someone around to confront him."

I was about to turn and look in the direction she mentioned when she grabbed my hand. "Turn now, and you'll spook him. Can you contact Jessie Shepard and see what he can do?" She gave me a pointed look.

"Oh, right? His unique talent." I wouldn't say he was a witch in this setting, but she was correct. Shepard was the best choice. "You wait here and keep an eye on the witness. I'm going inside and find Shepard so he can help. What's the guy wearing?"

"It looks like a white graphic tee shirt, but I

can't see what's on the front, and, I don't know if he's wearing shorts or pants because of the way he's partially hidden. But, he's definitely sporting a fedora-style hat."

I took her hand and tried to appear casual despite the body being loaded into an ambulance. "Have you noticed anyone else?"

"Oh, you're good at pretending to comfort me." With a smile for my eyes only, she said, "There are a couple of men I don't recognize sitting on a bench, but they could have seen who dropped our victim off."

"Agreed. Have the men interacted with each other? Do we need to bring them all in for questioning?"

"Yes, and yes." She kissed me. "I'm going to walk toward the bookstore, but I'll cast a spell to keep the men in the park. Jessie won't need backup to bring all three in for a chat."

"Lily, I don't want you anywhere near those men."

"I'm doing my civic duty. Think of me like

the chairwoman of the neighborhood watch committee."

"Then you'll head home?"

She lowered her glasses again, and her sable brown eyes twinkled. "Really?"

I shrugged. "Can't blame a guy for trying." We both knew there was no way she'd miss the chance to watch me question the men. Even if she was on the other side of the one-way mirror and couldn't ask any of her own. It was the best way to keep her out of harm's way.

Touching her arm, I said, "You'll be careful?"

Milo meowed, and I looked at Lily. "What did your familiar say?"

"That I was safer than you, since I'm quick with a wand."

"But you don't have your wand with you today. Do you?" I looked at her shorts, tee shirt, and deck shoes. There was no place to hide one.

"Remember, I learned magic without it.

The wand enhances a spell, nothing more. I've got the basics perfected."

Running a hand over Milo, I looked him in the eyes. "Keep her safe, and I'll get you an enormous fish of your own for dinner."

He butted his head against my hand, and I took that for a yes.

In a loud voice, I said, "All right, then. I'll see you later."

"Don't forget the ice cream." She strolled across the grass, avoiding the walkway.

I jogged up the front steps of the station and once I got inside, shouted for Shepard. He came out of the break room.

"Detective, is something wrong?"

"Lily spotted three men in the town square watching us with the victim. Would you encourage them to come in and answer a few questions?"

"You got it." He leaned forward before lowering his voice. "Can I use, well, you know?" He glanced around and whispered, "Magic."

"Hopefully, you won't need to. But Lily

will make sure they don't evade you, either." I knew he caught my drift.

"I'm on it." He stood straighter as he went out the back entrance in the same direction Lily had walked. He could sneak around the side of the square unnoticed.

"Alice, Shepard will bring in three witnesses. When Lily returns, can you take her to the observation area next to the small conference room? We'll use that to ask questions. Oh, and set out a few bottles of water. Our guests might be thirsty since they've been sitting in the hot sun."

"The room will be ready for you." She pushed back from the desk and walked down a short hallway to the kitchen, quickly returning with water bottles. She began wiping them down with alcohol wipes so that if we got lucky with a set of fingerprints, it would just be the witnesses.

With everything in motion, I returned to the front of the building and stopped at the bottom step. Mac and Peabody collected additional evidence and secured the area with crime scene tape. EL talked with Suzi, and Beth had finished closing the ambulance's back doors.

Casually, I glanced in the direction Lily had walked and scanned the bushes closest to the street. The man wearing the fedora was still watching us. He turned and spoke to another man who had left the bench, stretched, and joined him while looking at the sky and all around as if he wasn't paying attention to what was unfolding in front of them. It was then I felt his laser-like focus lock on me.

Shepard was about to be in position, and I was prepared to run if necessary. The honk of a horn drew my attention away from the men. A minivan skidded to a stop next to the ambulance. A woman, wearing a billowing sundress, an oversized hat, and dark round sunglasses, leaped out, leaving the driver's door open, and raced in our direction.

"Where is he?" she screamed as she tried to wrench open the ambulance doors.

I ran over and stepped in between her and the vehicle. "Ma'am, I'm Detective Erikson."

"I'm looking for Tom Holden. I got a phone call when I was at the Copper Kettle that said he was lying on the sidewalk, bleeding, and to get right over here." She looked around and screamed his name again when she saw the yellow tape surrounding the small yellow plastic markers. "Where is he? I need to talk to him."

"Ma'am. Who are you? How do you know Tom Holden?"

"I'm Simone, his wife. If you know what's good for you, open those doors so I can talk to him." Her lips formed a thin, hard line. "Now," came out more like a cornered animal's growl.

"May I see some identification?"

She glared at my team and me before striding to the van's passenger side. I followed her. She grabbed her bag and dumped the contents on the seat.

With the passenger door open, I could look inside. There was no sign of blood anywhere, and the items on the seat were typical of an oversized bag—a wallet, a book, lipstick, a hairbrush, and a medicine bottle. But there was one curious item: an empty Ziploc bag with a purple zipper, exactly like the bundles of cash in the evidence room.

Thrusting her license in my direction, she said, "Simone Holden. Now, can I see my Tom?"

"Mrs. Holden. I can't tell you for certain the man in the ambulance is your husband."

She jabbed her finger in the direction of the ambulance. "We should ask him."

"The man in the ambulance is deceased."

Her knees buckled, and I caught her before she crumpled to the cement. "What?"

"Yes, he was struck in the head, causing a fatal injury."

Wrenching her sunglasses off, her bloodshot gray eyes were saucer size. "Can I see him? Just to see if it's *really* him?"

"Come with me." I cupped my hand under

her elbow and supported her as she walked from the van to the ambulance.

"Dr. Dawson, Mrs. Holden believes her husband could be in the ambulance."

Suzi and Beth opened the back doors, and EL slid the gurney out. I said, "Mrs. Holden. I'm going to fold back the sheet. Take your time."

"Does he look dead?"

I wasn't sure how to answer that since I was certain she expected him to look the same as he had in life. "He may look different to you. But take your time."

Lifting the edge of the sheet on the side that hadn't been crushed, I paused. Her hand flew to her mouth, and an anguished cry slipped out in a horse whisper. "That's my Tom."

I replaced the sheet, and we stepped away from the ambulance, allowing EL to slide the gurney in and Suzi and Beth to do their job.

"He's going to the morgue. Tomorrow Dr. Dawson, the coroner, will perform an autopsy."

"Why? His head's bashed in; doesn't that confirm how he died?"

"Any time there is an unattended death, we need to be thorough." I gestured to the station. "Why don't we go inside and talk? A detective will move your van from the street to the parking area."

"All right." She allowed me to guide her up the stairs, glancing over her shoulder at the ambulance. I scanned the park and noticed the men were gone. Lily was jogging in my direction, glancing at the van. Hopefully Shepard had successfully detained the three men. Who knew? Maybe Mrs. Holden could shed some light on who they were and if there was a connection to her husband.

Once inside, she said, "May I use a rest room, please?"

Alice got up from the desk. "I'll take you." She walked Mrs. Holden down the hall and Lily burst into the lobby.

"Gage, who's the woman?"

"Simone Holden. She says our victim is Tom Holden, her husband."

She licked her lips. "Interesting. Did you get a look in the van?"

A quick glance in the direction Mrs. Holden had gone, I asked, "Why?"

Throwing up her hands, she said, "How did she end up at the exact spot where we found her husband dead? We need to consider she might be the person who dumped him."

Chapter 4
Lily

I sat in the observation room and thought about what I knew. Gage said there was no blood in the van, and supposedly, someone had called the woman about Mr. Holden lying on the sidewalk. I was skeptical, to say the least. One thing I had discovered since I began helping the Pembroke Cove Police Department and my dear Gage solve murders was that there was no such thing as a coincidence.

Jessie had convinced the three men watching the events unfold to come to the station and give a statement. Now, I'd watch the police question them in the room on the other side of this one-way mirror.

The door opened, and Gage came in. "I see Alice set you up." He looked around. "Did Milo come with you?"

"No. He said something about following the smell of fish. Look." I pointed to Jessie, gesturing to a chair.

"Have a seat, Mr. Andrus."

"Call me Felix." He took his hat off and ran his fingers through his hair, fluffing it up before he sat down.

"Too bad about the fella lying on the sidewalk. I saw the EMTs pull the sheet up. So, he's dead? May I?" He pointed to the bottles of water in the middle of the table.

Jessie didn't confirm or deny our victim's status. Instead, he said, "Help yourself. Can you tell me if you saw anyone other than the man on the sidewalk?"

He shook his head. "Nah, I heard a car door

slam and tires squeal, and that's what drew my attention to the guy."

"You didn't think to help?"

He leaned back in the chair. "I didn't want to get involved. You know, like if something bad was going down, getting caught in the crossfire was not in the best interest of my health."

"Did you hear a gunshot?"

"Nope. Was he shot to death?" He crossed his arms over his chest and looked at the small green light in the opposite corner, which indicated the cameras were rolling and he was being filmed. "Am I under suspicion, Officer?"

"This is a routine questioning of someone who may have seen or heard something that can help us solve the crime." Jessie paused for a moment. "Do you know a man, Tom Holden?"

I was glad I was focusing on Mr. Andrus. When the victim's name was mentioned, he flinched.

"Got ya." There was a connection. If Jessie missed it in person, it was on film.

Gage hurried out, and the next thing I

heard was the rap on the interview room door before it opened. He entered. "I'm Detective Erikson. Do you mind if I ask a couple of questions?"

Eyeing him carefully, Mr. Andrus said, "It's your time. I'm just here for the lobster and to do a little deep-sea fishing tomorrow. If that goes well, I hear there's a treasure hunting boat that will take folks out for a tour."

"When did you arrive in town?"

"A couple of days ago. My buddies and I needed to get away from our wives. We do this every June, pick a spot for fishing and good eating."

Gage nodded. "Fishing around these waters is pretty good. You mentioned treasure hunting; do you know there're rumors of sunken treasure from the pirate Black Sam Bellamy?"

The tension eased from Mr. Andrus's shoulders. "That's one reason we're in town. The lure of treasure." He winked at Gage. "But if we strike it rich, don't tell my wife."

"What have you done since you've arrived?"

He took a long drink of water and set the bottle aside. "We've eaten at the Clam Shack. Good lobster bisque and those dinner rolls? Perfection. We did a little kayaking yesterday and early in the morning today. That rental place at the marina has good kayaks. Have you been?"

Gage remained silent, which was one of his usual tactics to get a suspect chatting.

"If you haven't, it must be on your bucket list. We were hoping to spot a shark or two, but from what a local said, most times, the great whites don't make it up here until August or September. Too bad, we were hoping for a safe encounter."

"How far out did you kayak?"

He stroked a scruff of a beard. "A couple hundred yards, maybe more, maybe less. I'm not sure. The water was pretty calm yesterday, so we might have gone out further. One of my buddies might know. Do you want me to ask them?"

"No need. I can check," Jessie said.

"Did you notice anything out of the ordinary this morning while you were around town?"

"No. Like I told this officer, we heard a car screech away from the curb and that piqued our curiosity. But I didn't catch the make or model of the car. Sorry."

Mr. Andrus didn't look sorry, but I noted that. I needed Gage to ask where he was staying.

He glanced at the mirror and said, "You're staying a few more days at the..."

"We're at the B & B just down the street until Saturday morning."

"Mr. Andrus, we'll be in touch. Please let us know if you think of anything else you might have seen or heard." Gage handed him a business card.

He stashed it in the pocket of his shorts. "I'm free to leave?"

"You are. Officer Shepard will see you out." After the door was closed, Gage flicked open an evidence bag, placed the half-empty water bottle inside, sealed it, and put it in a cabinet on the other side of the room.

One down, two more potential suspects, and, of course, the widow. How would Gage get all the questioning done without keeping everyone waiting too long? More importantly, I'd be a witness to all of them.

The door to the room opened again. Sharon escorted Mrs. Holden inside. She clung to a packet of tissues and took off her hat to reveal short, dark hair.

"Mrs. Holden, please take a seat." Sharon sat next to her. Being close may provide comfort and help Gage extract important details.

"You and your husband are vacationing in Pembroke Cove?"

She nodded. "We arrived on Wednesday to get a beach vacation in before the summer's over. Tom loves the sand, salt air, and sun." She dropped her head and sniffed. "Loved."

"Do you know anyone in town?"

She lifted her head. "How would we? We're on vacation. It's not like we're here for a business meeting." She blew her nose and looked around. Sharon picked up a trash can and handed it to her. She dropped the used tissue inside.

Then she settled against the chair back. Mrs. Holden lifted her face to Gage. She crossed her arms over her chest with a sharp thrust to her chin. "How long will it take for you to find the person who killed my husband?"

"Mrs. Holden, we can't predict how long it would take to close an investigation, but I promise we'll do our best to get answers for you."

She dabbed her eyes with a fresh tissue. "This is so...distressing."

I couldn't help but wonder, did Simone Holden look like she was *distressed* other than her crying? Yes, she claimed to be the deceased's wife, but did we know if the man's name was Tom Holden? At this moment, it was her word about his identity.

Gage asked, "Can you tell me what happened leading up to when you arrived at the scene?"

"We had a tiff, and he stormed off. We're staying at the cute bed-and-breakfast a short walk from here. Anyway, we argued, and I took the van and went for a drive to clear my head. If I had known he was about to," she gulped, "expire, I wouldn't have fought with him over anything."

"May I ask what your disagreement was about?"

"Going fishing. He wanted to, and I get seasick, but he wanted us to be a Velcro couple on this vacation."

Gage's brows knitted together. "I'm not sure I understand."

"He wanted us to do all the same activities. I was sure he could hook up with other amateur fishermen at the marina and enjoy the morning or afternoon on the water. I told him I'd sit on the beach and read while he was off having fun."

"And he didn't like that idea?" Peabody asked.

With a slight shake of her head, she said, "No. Instead of talking it out, I got in the van and took off."

"Can anyone vouch for the argument or where you drove to?" Gage had a pad of paper and a pencil ready to write down anything that corroborated her story.

Her mouth gaped open. "Are you saying I'm a suspect in my Tom's death?" She slapped her hand on the table and jumped up. "This is an outrage. I want to call my lawyer."

"Mrs. Holden. I'm trying to establish a timeline for your husband leading up to the events that brought him to the walkway in front of the police station. If we can pinpoint the exact time he was last seen with you and someone overheard your argument, that will give us a starting point. Who might have seen him after you left?"

"Oh." She sat down in the chair with slumped shoulders. "Maybe the desk clerk heard us fighting. We were on the front porch. For that matter, anyone could have overheard us." Color flushed her cheeks. "We weren't subtle."

Was it possible to fake a blush from embarrassment? I couldn't take my eyes off Mrs. Holden. One minute, I thought she was a heartbroken wife, and the next, I thought she was lying. I texted Nikki to ask if she knew if Mabel was working the front desk for Donnie White at the Pembroke Cliffs Bed & Breakfast.

I got a quick response. *I'll find out. Give me a few.*

Gage said, "Getting back to you leaving. Did you stop for gas or maybe a coffee?"

"Detective Erikson, I was too distraught to get a coffee. As soon as I realized it was stupid to fight over a fishing trip, I figured I could take a bunch of those pills for seasickness and maybe even get one of the pressure point patches and enjoy time with Tom." Tears hovered on her lower lashes. "If only I could do things over."

He gave her a sympathetic nod. "I understand."

"When can I leave? I want to make arrangements to take Todd home."

Sharon swiveled in her chair. "Todd?"

She dabbed her eyes with a fresh tissue. "Sorry. That was my pet name for him."

"Didn't you say you were at the Copper Kettle when you received a phone call about your husband in front of the police station?"

Tossing a crumbled tissue in the trash can, she said, "Right, the Copper Kettle."

Gage handed her a card. "If you think of anything else, please don't hesitate to call me. Once I know when we're able to release your husband's body, I'll be in touch. It could be several days."

She sucked her lips in. "Thank you." Standing, she extended her hand to shake his. "I guess you know how to find me."

"Yes, ma'am, I do."

Sharon escorted her out. He looked at me even though he couldn't see me through the mirrored glass. Tipping his head to one side, he said, "I'm sure you heard the entire conversation. I hope you took notes."

Jessie escorted the next man from the town square into the room. He glanced nervously from side to side and stared at the green light in the corner. "Is that, that, a camera, and you're recording me?"

"Yes, Mr.?"

"Capes, first name Eddie." He pulled out a seat and sat down. "This won't take long, and I know the drill. This isn't my first time being questioned by the fuzz. I'm kinda unlucky when it comes to being an unsuspecting bystander."

"Really." Gage leaned forward. "Tell me what you saw today."

He nodded and swallowed so hard that the muscles in his neck bulged. "That lady that just walked through the lobby. I heard her fighting with the dead guy this morning when I was having breakfast at the inn."

"Do you know what they were fighting about?"

"Her being seasick yesterday. She told him she wasn't gettin' back on a boat for love nor money. He could go suck lemons. Then she stormed off, and he came into the dining room. He poured himself a mug of joe and sat down. He was still there when I left for the park."

"Have you ever seen either of these people before?"

"Nope. Well, I mean, I've seen them the last few days hanging around the inn, and we've crossed paths at a couple of restaurants, but there's nothin' to speak of."

"Did you happen to hear the lady call the man by his name?"

He tipped his head back and closed his eyes. Scrunching up his face, he said, "Terry?" He looked at Gage and then Jessie. "Sorry, I wasn't paying attention. I try to stay out of other people's business. If you catch my drift."

Gage nodded. "Did you notice anything when you were in the town square?"

"Nah, but I heard a car door slam and tires screech. You know, like someone was speeding away super fast."

"Mr. Capes."

He gave a toothy grin. "Call me Eddie. Mr. Capes is my pop."

Gage gave another nod but didn't use his first name. "Do you have plans to leave town?"

"Not until I know how this turns out. This is better than reality TV. Ya know being this close to a real live murder."

With a cocked brow, Gage said, "Why do you think it's murder?"

Eddie Capes leaned closer and tapped the end of his nose. "Cuz, you wouldn't be so curious about everything that happened this morning if it weren't."

I'd give Gage a ton of credit. He never betrayed his feelings about these types of conversations. I wanted to remind the witness to stop acting smug.

"And before you think Willy can tell you something different, his eyes are terrible. He can only see really good far away, or maybe it's up close. Either way, questioning him will be a waste of time."

Jessie said, "I'll escort you to the lobby."

Gage stood. "Thank you, Eddie." He held up his index finger and shrugged his shoulders, and in walked the third man with Sharon.

The older gentleman bumped into the chair and righted it before it could crash to the floor. "Sorry," he mumbled.

"Have a seat."

The man pulled out a bottle of hand sanitizer and squirted it. While he rubbed his hands together, he said, "I'll cut right to the end for you. My name is Wilbur Christy. I didn't kill that man, but I'm pretty sure I know who did." He pulled out the chair, and the legs scraped against the floor.

Mr. Christy pointed for Gage and Sharon to sit down. "I'm only gonna explain this once, so you'd best have your video recording me. I'm not going down for whacking that guy."

Chapter 5
Lily

I took a step closer to the glass. Not that I needed to hear better since his voice was coming through the speaker loud and clear. I wanted to see his facial expressions, and the truth would be in his eyes. Judging by the deep wrinkles that lined his face, I'd guess Wilbur Christy was near seventy, a significant difference between him, Eddie Capes, and Felix Andrus. They had been closer to forty. I guessed the current witness was approximately the same age as the victim and Simone.

"Mr. Christy. Would you care to explain

your statement?" Gage nodded to Sharon, who sat across from the suspect. "Officer Peabody can get you a coffee if you'd like."

"I'll take a water. It was hot sitting in that park." Sharon handed him a bottle. "But this won't take long. Simone killed him." He drank half the bottle and nodded his thanks to Sharon. "I've known all of them for around twenty years. Although Felix and Eddie might have hot heads, Tom's get-rich-quick schemes tested Simone's patience every day. Today, sell vitamins; tomorrow, some other hair-brained idea."

I thought of the bag full of money. Financial constraints in a marriage would make any couple nervous. But to kill? That didn't seem likely.

"Now, take note. She loved him something fierce, but her temper was worse than anyone I've ever seen. She'd be fine one minute and throwing plates or whatever was handy the next."

Gage was taking notes but not asking questions. This interrogation was best left to unravel organically.

"Tom and Simone had a huge row this morning. At one point, she even said, and I quote, *I could kill you and dump your body over the edge of that stupid boat you want to go fishing on, and you can permanently swim with them.*"

For a man who had potentially witnessed a life-ending argument, Wilbur Christy was very calm about it. I wondered if his statement was fact with a healthy dose of fiction. Simone had seemed genuinely distraught when she learned her husband had died.

I scratched my neck.

But had she? Looking back, 'she'd been upset but not disbelieving or in shock. Wouldn't that have been the expected reaction?

"Now, I didn't say that."

Dang, I missed Gage's question.

"You implied that Simone could have thrown something at Tom and caused his death."

"She has a good arm. If she meant to hit him, she would have, but I didn't see her throw nothing at him today."

With the potential murder weapon now in EL's lab, he'd discover the truth. Either Tom Holden was killed and left in front of the station, or he was assaulted nearby. But there was a trail of blood drops from the street up the walkway to consider.

"Did you see anyone on the street or hear anything?"

Mr. Christy looked at Sharon. "I'm sure the others told you about the car door and tire squeal. From where I was sitting, I couldn't see a thing. Felix was the one keeping watch in the bushes. I think he got nervous after the sound of the tires chirping on the pavement. The timing's a little fuzzy. I didn't sleep well last night, too much silence. I'm from Boston." He tapped the top of the table. "You should write that down, too. We all live within five miles of each other."

"Mr. Christy. How can you be sure that Mrs. Holden killed her husband?"

He finished the rest of the water bottle, put the cap back on, and placed it on the table in front of him. Looking at Gage, he said, "Love, money, and revenge. Simone's motive is neatly packaged. She loved and hated her husband at the same time. With him dead, she gets his money and revenge for all the times she gave in and did things to make him happy. I'd say she's going to be a very merry widow."

"Can you vouch for Mr. Andrus and Mr. Capes' whereabouts for the morning?"

He nodded. "We had breakfast at the inn where we're staying. Wandered around town trying to decide what to do next, and we got a coffee at a bakery before meandering into the park."

I made a note to check with William about the coffee. Then, my phone vibrated with an incoming text. Mabel Thorpe was working at the inn today. I could swing by there on my way to the bakery. I texted back. *Thanks.*

"Do you have plans to leave town, Mr. Christy?"

The man grinned. "Are you kidding? I know how this goes. Stay in town until the local police department permits us to leave. Honestly, I'm going to enjoy watching you arrest that woman. She's been a thorn in Tom's side for years. Finally, she'll get what's coming to her. She's going to look good in prison gray." He stood, picked up his empty water bottle, and said, "I'm around." He didn't wait for Sharon to get up. "I'll see myself out the door."

She was one step behind him as he left the room.

Since that was the last interview, I exited the observation area and rounded the corner. Gage pushed out the chair next to him, and I sat down.

"What did you think?"

I chewed the corner of my lip and processed the information from each person. "I'm sure someone is already looking at the security footage for the front of the building, so the car that the three men all say was there needs to be found."

"And Mr. Christy's statement that Simone Holden is guilty?"

"It's easy to blame the wife. But when I glanced into the van, there wasn't a drop of blood. If she'd struck him before dumping him here, there should be."

Gage's brows knitted together. "Why drop him here, of all places?"

"Do you think he was still alive? Maybe whoever did that thought he'd get help quicker than trying to take him to an emergency room— and don't forget, we believe the murder weapon was deliberately dropped."

"Or left."

I said, "Can I see your notes?"

He slid the notebook to me. As I scanned them, I discovered we were on the same track with no direction to a conclusion. "What if the three men did it together?"

"It's possible." He sent a text. "I've asked

Mac if he discovered anything on the surveillance tape."

"The angle is right to see the entire street, correct?"

Gage said, "Yes, but we both know people are sly and have figured out how to evade cameras."

Mac came around the corner, his face grim. "Gage, I've reviewed footage from all our cameras. Our victim stumbled up the walk, dropped what looks like a rock and fell to the ground."

"We've had reports of a car door slamming and tires screeching on the road. Any chance you got the make and model?"

"Boss, I scanned the tape a half hour before and after Lily discovered our vic. There wasn't a car that was stopped on the street and then sped away."

Gage looked at me. "The only positive is they all know how to lie straight to my face without so much as a flinch." He shook his head. "I'm going to the lab to see if EL has discovered anything. You can take the truck and I'll meet you at your place."

I gave him a quick kiss. "No need. I'll have Nikki pick me up."

He narrowed his eyes. "Lily, where are you going?"

I decided to tell him since I'd have the clue board up and filled out by the time he got home. "I'm going to swing by the bed-and-breakfast and talk with Mabel and then check out the coffee alibi with William." I gave him a peck on the lips. "Don't worry, nothing dangerous. Just a little information gathering."

He took my hand. "Would it do any good to ask you to let me question people?"

"Nope, and one of these days, you're not even going to ask me that question, but accept that I can discover things you can't. You realize people get intimidated talking to a police officer or a detective. You've all perfected that scowl."

Gage looked at Mac. "Do we scowl?"

He said, "Boss, often we look stern; it comes

with the job, and it helps ferret out the bad guys."

I laughed. "Sometimes? My tactics are more fruitful." My fingers trailed over Gage's shoulders as I walked behind him and out the door.

He called after me, "Be careful."

"Always."

I sent Nikki a text. *Want to meet me at the B & B?*

A quick response caused me to chuckle. *I'm on the porch.*

That witch was one step ahead of me, like an excellent partner in crime should be.

I hurried down the sidewalk, giving the crime scene tape a wide berth. A ripped corner of paper lay in the grass near the tree line. I bent over and stretched out my hand, but when I saw it was part of a one-hundred-dollar bill I paused, looked around to see if I was being watched, and then magicked a Ziplock bag like Gage used for evidence and slipped the triangle inside. I'd give it to him later. I continued to the inn.

Nikki and Steve were gliding on the porch swing as I climbed the wide wooden steps. "Hey guys. Just hanging around?"

Steve grinned. "Spending time with my favorite girl and wherever she wants to go is fine with me."

Occasionally, Steve had accompanied us while we hunted for clues. He was with us the day Nikki rescued Gage's Great Dane, Brutus, after his owner had been killed. I smiled as I remembered Steve scrunched into the back seat of my mini Coop and Brutus taking up the other two-thirds.

"Let's talk to Mabel, and then we need to swing by the Sweet Spot."

Nikki stood and Steve said, "I'll wait for you here. No sense in overwhelming the poor woman. She's had much to deal with since St. Patrick's Day."

That was true. Donnie White had hired her

to manage the inn while he was taking treasure hunters on charters. I pulled open the screen door, and we entered the pristine lobby. The scent of lemon polish and coffee mingled. Around the corner, Mabel was working at the front desk.

She looked up and smiled. "Hi, girls. How are you and what can I do for you today?"

Mabel called everyone girls or boys no matter how old or young they were, and it was endearing.

Leaning against the wooden counter, I said, "Good, thanks for asking. And you?"

"Busy day, but summers usually are in town. It's a blessing that scandal didn't close this place down." She gave Nikki a sad smile. "You poor girl. What you went through for your wedding? It was just a shock."

"Steve and I are happily married, and we hang on to the wonderful memories of that time."

She patted Nikki's hand. "Good for you. Now, how can I help today?"

No sense in beating around the cauldron. "I'm not sure if you heard, but there was a tragic accident earlier. Tom Holden was killed."

Her face went slack. "Tom Holden?"

"Yes, he was staying here with his wife, Simone? They checked in a few days ago."

She nodded. "Yes, they argue a lot." With a furtive glance around the room, she dropped her voice and tapped her temple. "In here I call them the Bickersons."

I didn't understand the reference, and it must have shown on my face.

"It was an old radio and television program about a married couple who bicker all the time." She smiled. "I love the oldies. A simpler time."

Now it made sense. "They argued often?"

Mabel folded her arms on top of the counter. "From the moment they walked onto the front porch. I swear, I've heard no one pick at their spouse as much. Poor man."

"Did you hear them arguing today?"

"Oh yes. All about going fishing. She said no, and he said they had to go. Something about finally pulling out a big trophy."

Nikki said, "If he were trying to get a trophy fish, they'd need to go much further out, into open water."

"Right, and Simone said she got seasick, which is why she didn't want to go."

"Mabel, did you hear anything else that might be interesting?"

"Only that she didn't want to waste another day on a boat." After she said, *tsk tsk*, she continued, "That poor woman. Even if you fight with your husband, it's heartbreaking to lose him."

"Has she come back to the inn since she left?"

"Left? Why, Simone Holden is sitting in the parlor. It was Mr. Holden who stormed off."

My eyes widened. "Are you sure?"

"Of course I am. She's been reading and drinking tea. I asked her if she wanted to sit on the porch but she was comfortable in there. You know, the view of the flower garden is breathtaking."

I looked at Nikki with eyes wide, and she looked at me. "Thank you, Mabel. We'll go pay our respects."

Clasping Nikki's arm, I whispered, "Let's not mention anything about Tom. I have a niggling feeling this case is about to take a sharp turn."

We walked into the room and stopped. A young woman with long dark hair was reading a copy of Rebecca, wearing tan linen shorts and a lavender silk blouse.

"Hello." I walked into the space. "Isn't this a lovely room?"

She closed the book and put it on her lap. "It certainly is." When she looked at me, I noticed the intense blue color of her eyes, and her ivory skin was flawless. With a glance out the window, she said, "The gardens provide such a sense of peace. I've enjoyed our trip here.

When my husband mentioned he wanted to vacation in this small town, I wasn't sure I would. But he promised me oysters and lobster. How could I say no?"

"Indeed." Nikki crossed the room and extended her hand. "This is Lily Michaels. She owns the local bookstore, and I'm Nikki. I bake for the inn and the restaurants in town."

"It's wonderful to meet you both—and if those scones came from your kitchen that I enjoyed earlier today, kudos. They're some of the best I've ever had."

Glancing around the room, I said, "Where's your husband?"

A frown graced her mouth. "I'm not sure. We had a minor disagreement about another day of fishing, and he stalked off." She looked at the diamond-encrusted watch on her delicate wrist. "He should be back by now." She got up. "If you'll excuse me, I'm going to our room and give him a call."

Should I stop her and tell her what had happened? But that wasn't my place.

"It was lovely to meet you both. Enjoy your day."

Nikki looked at me, and I withdrew my phone from my pocket. "Gage needs to hear about the second Mrs. Holden.

Chapter 6
Gage

When Lily's name popped up on my cell, I answered it. "Hi." There was so much more behind a simple two-letter word. I waited.

"You need to come to the inn. There's a woman here who Mabel said is Simone Holden, but she's not the woman we met earlier."

I put my hand on the doorjamb and hung my head. "Are you saying a fake Mrs. Holden identified our victim?"

"Potentially. Nikki and I'll wait on the

porch with Steve. If she tries to leave, I'll find a way to detain her until you arrive."

"Be there as fast as I can." I pocketed the phone and yelled for Peabody. As if by magic, my detective appeared in the doorway.

"We have a problem. There's a second Mrs. Holden at the inn. I need you to come with me to interview her."

She expressed no emotion and said, "There's a wrinkle I wasn't expecting. I'll update Mac. Should he come with us or get the report from EL and meet us there?"

"Have him check in with EL, then meet us at the inn. Let them know it is possible we don't have a proper identification of the victim. We might bring a second Mrs. Holden to identify the body. That is, if she can provide concrete proof, she's who she says she is." I lifted my hand and rubbed it over my head. What else could happen on a lazy Sunday? With any luck, we'd interview the second Mrs. Holden and get to Lily's place by mid-afternoon.

. . .

Since I hoped to go from the B & B to Lily's, I drove my truck and parked it in front of the inn. Peabody was on her motorcycle. Lily, Nikki, and Steve were sitting on the porch. To the casual observer, it would seem they were enjoying a summer afternoon. But the tip of Lily's head in the direction of the front door to the inn told me she was ready to spring into action if needed.

Rising from the chair, she met me at the top of the stairs. "Hi. Our lady is still inside. She went to her room to call her husband and hasn't come down yet."

"What was your impression?" I lifted a hand in greeting to Nikki and Steve.

"She was relaxed, absorbed in her book, and not at all anxious. Mabel said she never left the inn after the argument with her husband."

"What about slipping out the back?" I wasn't as familiar with the inn as Lily. She had spent a lot of time here for Nikki and Steve's wedding and when we were investigating the death of a guest.

"The only exit for the parlor is into the garden, which doesn't have a gate to the street. She'd have to walk past Mabel to leave."

I frowned. "That's not quite accurate, remember there's that back exit to the garage off the dining room."

"True. But whoever killed Tom might have dirt or even blood on their clothes. I'll ask Mabel if she remembers what Simone was wearing when she was fighting with her husband."

"Good idea."

Peabody joined us, and we crossed the wide porch, entering the lobby. Nikki and Steve remained as lookouts on the porch. I figured they could detain her just in case the woman got past us.

Lily walked to the desk. "Hey, Mabel. I'm sorry to bother you again, but I was wondering, do you remember what Mrs. Holden was wearing when she was arguing with her husband?"

"I sure do." She nodded at me and smiled at

Peabody. "A pair of light-colored linen shorts and a silky blouse in a pale shade of purple—nothing like what you'd expect someone to wear going to the beach for the day, a nice out-to-dinner outfit. But she'd need a sweater or something. You know how the restaurants keep the air conditioners on high most days. And, of course, sandals."

I wanted to ask more questions, but Mabel's gaze fixed on the area behind us and said, "Mrs. Holden."

I turned. She looked very different than the other woman. Dark, cascading hair fell around her shoulders, framing her delicate features. She was thin and dressed as Mabel had described.

She gave us a small smile. "Hello. Mabel, when Tom comes back, would you let him know that I'm in the parlor?"

"I certainly will."

Lily stepped forward. "You weren't able to reach him?"

The woman frowned. "No, it went straight to voicemail, which is odd. He always has it on. He must be still working off his mad."

I guessed that meant he wasn't ready to speak with his wife. "Mrs. Holden, I'm Detective Erikson." I flashed her my badge. "And this is my colleague, Detective Peabody. May we speak with you for a moment?"

She licked her lips and looked at Lily, the only slightly familiar person in the group.

Lily said, "Why don't we go into the parlor and talk in private?" She took Mrs. Holden's arm and escorted her into the sun-drenched room.

Peabody followed me inside and closed the door.

"What's wrong? Has something happened to my husband?" As she was asking questions, she perched on the edge of the sofa, her eyes blinking rapidly.

I took the chair across from the couch, and Lily sat beside her. "We believe he might have collapsed in front of the police station earlier today."

"What? No." Her voice cracked and her hand flew to her mouth. "He's out taking a walk. It's what he always does when we quarrel. It doesn't mean anything. We take some time to cool down then kiss and make up. It's our way."

"Can you tell me what your husband was wearing when he left the inn?"

She nodded. "He's thin and tall, wearing a pink polo shirt with a blue stripe on the colllar and arms, navy blue shorts, and white Keds sneakers. The kind you slip on. Also, he has blond hair, and he didn't shave this morning, light blue eyes, and he's got a nasty-looking scar on his right knee. It was from a fishing spear or something just as dangerous that got him in the leg."

As she described the man in the morgue, my next question would be more difficult. "Ma'am, could you show me your driver's license, passport, or anything that can confirm your identity?"

Her eyes grew even more prominent, if it was possible. "Why? I'm Simone Holden."

I nodded. "Please, ma'am, if you don't mind. Detective Peabody can accompany you to your room while you retrieve it."

"Am I in trouble?" She looked from me to Lily as tears filled her eyes. "This won't end well, will it?"

"Ma'am." Peabody was standing now. "If you prefer, I can go upstairs and get your bag."

Her eyes narrowed. "I need to see your identification for more than a split second. How do I know you're really police officers?"

I withdrew my badge from my pocket and passed it to her. Mac slipped into the room and stood near the door.

She looked at the badge, scrutinized my identification, looked back at me, and then scanned it again. Repeating this process with Peabody's badge, she stood tall and walked out of the room. "Come with me."

Once I heard their footsteps on the stairs, I looked at Mac. "First impressions?"

"It depends on her identification. If they look legit, we need to run her down to the morgue to positively identify the body."

He was right. "Why didn't I study the other Simone's ID more closely?"

"Who would lie about being a spouse?" Lily looked at us both. "That's not something anyone would expect."

"Her description matches the body in EL's morgue."

"I'm taking a leap here. But if he is Tom Holden, and if this woman is his wife, who is and how do we find the fake Simone?"

"Fingerprints?"

Thinking back to the interviews, I realized she hadn't drunk from a water bottle, but she had blown her nose. DNA could help us discover who she was. It took days, sometimes weeks, to get a positive match, and it could mean never if she wasn't in a database. "No, she didn't touch anything."

Voices getting louder drew my attention. The woman and Peabody entered the parlor again, and she closed the door.

"Detective, my credentials." She flipped open her wallet, handing it to me along with her passport. Her voice was sharp, and I understood her tone. If someone had challenged my identity I would have felt the same way.

"Thank you, Mrs. Holden. We needed to move cautiously."

She dropped to the sofa. "You have bad news."

"I'm sorry to tell you, but I believe your husband died this morning in front of the police station. I'd like for you to come with us to the morgue."

Clasping her hands together, she looked me directly in the eye. "Tom is dead?" Tears filled her large blue eyes, spilling over her lashes unchecked down her cheeks. "How did it happen? Did he have a heart attack? I tried to get him to eat better, kick the fried foods and ice cream."

"We believe he was the victim of an assault."

An anguished sob came from the depths of her soul and filled the room. It was gut-wrenching. Lily slipped her arm around Simone's shoulders and held the woman while she cried.

I hesitated to speak, unsure how long to wait before asking her to come with me.

Bobbing her head toward the door, she said, "Gage, I wonder if we could give Simone some privacy."

"Don't go." She clung to Lily like a life preserver in the middle of the Atlantic.

"I'm not going anywhere." Her words were soothing.

Mac and Peabody stood, and I followed them out of the room. Lily would prepare Mrs. Holden for what we needed to do next.

The minutes ticked by, and the sounds of crying lessened. I sat on the bottom stair, my hands clasped and head down. This was the worst part of my job informing loved ones.

Peabody knelt next to me. "Boss, I'll call EL

and let him know we'll be in with the real Mrs. Holden."

"Fine. I'm not sure what time, but yeah." Rubbing my hand over my face, I said, "Run by the station, get the discarded tissues from our Jane Doe and the water bottle Felix Andrus left behind. It's in the cabinet. We need to process them and learn all we can."

"What about the bottles from Eddie Capes and Wilbur Christy?"

"That cagey one? Christy took the bottle with him." I shook my head. Had there been a way I could have stopped that? It had happened so fast.

"And Eddie Capes?"

"Like the fake Mrs. Holden, he never touched anything." I rubbed my hand over my chin. "What do they all have in common that they're trying to hide?"

"Good question, but we'll find out. We always do." Peabody stood tall. "I'll see you at the morgue."

"Mac, you're with me. We need to chat

with Mabel about our three other gentlemen and our Jane Doe."

I glanced at the parlor door and wondered how long it would take Lily to get Mrs. Holden ready to face the harsh reality that her husband was dead.

Mabel smoothed her hand over the front of her blouse and licked her lips. Her eyes darted around the room. Finally, she said, "Detectives, the three men staying here are perfectly lovely. Their rooms are tidy, and their table manners are impeccable. If you ask me, they're the perfect example of the type of people we want vacationing in Pembroke Cove."

"Did you see them interact with Mr. and Mrs. Holden?"

She looked at the ceiling and pursed her lips. "Not that I recall. But I saw them chatting with a pretty woman on the front porch when I left."

Could this be a break? "Is she a guest here? Can you describe her?" There was hope that this lead could pan out for us.

"She's not a guest here. I thought I heard her mention something about staying at the Coastal Motel, but maybe I didn't. She was average height, had short dark hair, and the nicest laugh. The four of them were talking about going to Robin's Café for drinks."

"Did you see them leave?" Mac asked.

"No. Donnie was home by three, and he took over the inn. I was leaving late since I got behind on some laundry. The B & B's been very busy this summer."

"Thanks, Mabel. If you think of anything else, be sure to let me or Mac know."

Standing tall with her eyes bright, she said, "You can count on me."

"Gage? Simone's ready."

I noticed the poor woman had gone from a vibrant, cheerful lady to a shell of a person. My gut clenched when I thought how hard it would be for her to see her husband draped in a sheet on the metal slab.

We walked out to the porch, and my police-issued sedan was curbside. I needed to thank Peabody for going above and beyond on this one.

I opened the back door. Lily and Mrs. Holden slid over the hard plastic seat. Mac got in front on the passenger side, and I'd make the five-minute drive.

Lily said, "Mrs. Holden, if you have questions, just ask. We want to help you in any way we can."

"You've been so kind, Lily. Are you a police officer, too?"

"No, remember I mentioned I own the bookstore?"

"Oh, right."

I could see in my rearview mirror she was staring out the window. I couldn't imagine what she might be feeling. The anxiety of telling us it was her husband must weigh heavy on her heart. However, it wouldn't bring us closer to who attacked him. If EL was right and that rock was the weapon, it could give us a valuable clue.

I parked next to the sidewalk, and we silently entered the morgue-containing building. EL waited for us in the lobby. He approached Mrs. Holden and shook her hand.

"I'm Dr. Dawson. If you'll come with me, I'll make this as painless as possible."

Mrs. Holden allowed herself to be led into an interior room. At the threshold, she stopped. "Lily, will you come with me?"

"Yes." She glided across the room and crooked her arm through Simone's.

We entered the cool, brightly lit room, and in the center was a stretcher with a sheet draped over it. Mrs. Holden clasped Lily's hand, inhaled slowly, and exhaled even slower.

She nodded to EL. "I'm ready."

He slowly folded back the sheet just enough so that she would view the uninjured portion of his face. She took a step closer, and her face screwed up.

"Can I see his right knee?"

"Simone," Lily asked, "what's wrong?"

EL did as she requested and exposed the man's knees. I leaned in. No scar.

Mrs. Holden was staring at me. "This is not my husband."

Chapter 7
Lily

I couldn't believe what Simone had said, but she was lucid and fully aware, as the death grip on my hand indicated. Viewing a dead body was traumatizing. "Simone, I don't understand."

Her grip relaxed as she stepped back from the body and bolted for the door. Once we were in the lobby, she said, "He sort of looks like my Tom, but he doesn't have a scar on his knee, and this man is chubbier." Her face brightened. "Does this mean my husband's alive?"

I wasn't sure how to answer that question,

and luckily, I didn't have to since Gage had just heard the entire conversation.

"Mrs. Holden, are you sure?"

"I should know my husband." Her voice would have raised a vampire at midday. "I'm telling you, that isn't him. So, the only question is, can you take me back to the inn so I'll be there when he arrives? I wouldn't want him to worry if Mabel tells him I left with several police officers." She whirled on her heel and flung open the main door. It banged against the wall before it slammed shut.

Gage said, "This has never happened before. We have a dead Mr. Doe and a phantom Mrs. Doe."

"Are fingerprints going to be your best method of identification?"

"Without a positive ID, yes, we'll need to rely on prints from everyone. It's too bad we're missing a couple of sets." Sharon, EL, and Mac had followed us into the lobby.

Gage gave them a long look. "As crazy as all this is, nothing about this case can't wait until tomorrow. We'll return Mrs. Holden to the B & B and we can gather at Lily's. I know she's itching to get her clue board out and start making notes."

I nodded. "Give us thirty minutes. I want to swing by the Sweet Spot."

Sharon's eyes sparkled. "Cupcakes?"

That wasn't why I wanted to see William, but it was an excellent cover. "I'll get what I can."

EL kissed Sharon. "I'll meet you there? I have a couple of things to finish up here."

She told him she'd wait.

Mac said, "I'll stop at my place and pick up Margeret and the baby. Then we'll be along."

Now that the plans were confirmed, Mac, Gage, and I climbed into the sedan where Simone Holden was waiting for us.

The drive to the inn was silent. My heart constricted when I thought of all that she had been through today, including the argument with her husband. He didn't answer her call, and the viewing of the body, which thankfully hadn't been her Tom, must have been taxing.

We stopped next to the curb. Simone turned in the back seat and looked at each of us. I guessed it was to make sure she had our attention.

"I don't hold you responsible for what happened today. But I'm curious, who identified that man as my husband?"

"A woman at the scene claimed she was Mrs. Holden and said it was Tom Holden."

Her eyes narrowed. "Did she give you proof of her claim?"

"I glanced at her ID. The picture was the same. I've never had a person lie to me about being related to a victim."

"Now you have." She turned away. "There's been a woman I've bumped into regularly since I got to town. I brushed it off as a small-town coincidence, but is there really such a thing?"

Without waiting for an answer, she said, "I took a selfie at this cute coffee shop and made sure to get her in the background. I think it was at the Copper Kettle." She withdrew her phone and scrolled through the images. She handed Gage her cell. "That's her."

I leaned over his shoulder and wasn't surprised to see the woman who claimed to be Simone. Gage showed Mac next.

"Mrs. Holden, would you mind if I texted myself this picture?"

"Do what you need to do." She shuddered. "It makes my skin crawl knowing she impersonated me, and you didn't need to say a word. The lack of conversation confirmed that something is wrong." She glanced at the inn as the front door swung open.

A tall, handsome blond man ran down the steps, his arms wide. "Simone."

Mac jumped out and opened her door as she leapt into the man's arms with a cry, "Tom." She pulled back and studied his face. "I thought you were dead." Cupping his face in her hands, she showered him with kisses and murmurs of apology.

The man holding Simone in his arms was dressed exactly like the man I had found outside the police station, right down to the Keds sneakers. It was uncanny.

He shushed her with soothing words and hugged her close. We closed the car doors and waited on the sidewalk for a few moments.

Gage cleared his throat. "Mr. Holden, may we speak with you for a moment?"

Simone slid to the ground but kept her arms wrapped around his waist.

"What's going on?" He looked at his wife. "When I returned to the inn, Mabel said you'd left with a couple of detectives and a bookstore owner. I was worried sick."

"I'm sorry. I tried to call, but you didn't answer your phone."

He pulled it from his pocket. "I forgot to charge it. I came right back when I realized it, but you were gone."

"Mr. Holden, I'm Detective Erikson. This is Detective Sullivan and Lily Michaels."

He gave a curt nod.

"There was an assault outside the police station this morning, and a woman claiming to be Simone Holden identified the victim as Tom Holden. We had no reason to believe it was false information until Lily stopped at the inn to check with Mabel."

"And you realized I was alive?"

Simone said, "Not exactly. After they realized something was wrong since there couldn't be two of me, this detective asked me to identify a man they believed was you." Her voice broke with emotion, and he wrapped his arms around her.

"Simy, I'm right here. Healthy as a stubborn mule."

She buried her face in his chest, and her shoulders pulled in as a protective barrier. Tom looked at Gage. "If there's nothing else, can I take my wife inside? You can see this has been overwhelming for her."

"Yes. But please don't leave town. Your wife took a picture of a woman who she thinks has been following her since you arrived. It's the woman who said she was Simone Holden."

His face went slack. "Are we—is she in danger? Maybe we should go home."

"I don't think you're in danger. I would like you to stay in town a couple of days until we can try to get this sorted out. And if at any time you feel unsafe, call the station or even myself." He handed Tom a card. "You can reach me twenty-four–seven."

"I don't know." His brow furrowed.

"Mr. Holden, enjoy the shops and eateries in town. Everyone is very nice, and the food is excellent everywhere, but stay together." I magicked a card from my shoulder bag, and before I handed it to him, I closed my eyes. "If you show this at any of the local restaurants, you'll receive a twenty-five percent discount."

He took the card and slipped it into his shorts pocket. Smiling, he nodded his thanks. "I won't leave the inn without it."

"That's what I hoped you'd say." I slipped

my hand into Gage's. "You two have a lot to talk about, but if you need anything, call Gage."

The couple climbed the painted porch steps with arms entwined around each other's waists. Nikki and Steve rose from the bench and waited until they were inside before joining us.

I kissed Gage's cheek. "Nikki and I'll be right back. We're going to get Sharon some cupcakes and check on William." I started to walk away and then turned. "Can you text me that picture of Ms. Doe? I want to see if William or Jill recognize her."

"Lily." The subtle tone in Gage's voice didn't slow my brain from spinning ideas or hatching my plan.

I heard Steve chuckle. "You know where they're going. Maybe we should stop at the market and get food not laden with butter and sugar."

Mac chuckled. "You figure it out and I'll see you later."

. . .

I did one last wave to Gage and Steve and told Nikki about everything that had happened, including the Tom Holden impersonator.

"So, you're saying even the clothes were the same?"

"Yes. Whatever is going on, there was a lot of thought put into John Doe's appearance."

The door to the Sweet Spot opened and a couple came out, dressed in beach cover-ups and flip flops, sipping iced coffee.

William was behind the counter when we entered. Jill Dilly was wiping down the bistro tables in the cafe section, and the bakery was empty of other customers.

"Good afternoon, ladies. How are my two favorite customers?" He winked, since if Jill hadn't been in the room, he would have said witches. His late wife, Lulu, had been a witch in our coven, but that was before I knew I was a witch.

"Hoping you have some delectable cupcakes, cookies, or whatever might make a good dessert tray for an impromptu cookout at my place."

His brow quirked. "Yesterday, you mentioned you were going fishing."

I laughed. "That seems like a lifetime ago. So much has happened since we got on the boat this morning." I pulled up the picture on my phone. "Have you seen this woman in the background? The one with the short, dark hair?"

He took the phone and looked at it closely before handing it back to me. "I think so. Over the last week, she's been coming in and getting a coffee, but she's usually with a few men, one older and two about her age. No one I recognize."

I wished I had a picture of the men from the town square. "Did three men come in earlier today and buy coffee?"

"Yes, and those are the same guys I saw with that lady, but she wasn't with them today."

Jill placed some trash in the can and asked if she could see the picture.

I handed it to her. "Do you recognize her?"

"Yes, she was in yesterday when William walked over to Tuckers. We needed lightbulbs. But she was with a chubby blond guy. He didn't say much; she did the ordering, he paid the check, and they left."

I gave Nikki a side eye, which connected our victim with the fake Mrs. Holden. "Thanks, Jill."

William had a large white pastry box open. "Should I just fill it with a variety?"

"Please." I wandered to the window. Though I had seen this view countless times, I wondered how those men were also connected to the dead man, not just the mystery lady. It was an educated guess he was one of the younger men in the group. I had so many thoughts floating around my head that I needed to write down the clues on my board to make sense of them.

"Here you go, Lily, and I added in the last of the cinnamon pecan buns."

I placed a hand over my heart. "You're too good to me, William."

A twinkle in his eye and his smile warmed me.

"You're so much like my Lulu, in all ways. I've told you before if we'd had a daughter, I can't help but think she'd have been just like you." He handed me the box of sweets, and I gave him my credit card.

"If those men and the lady return, would you let me or Gage know?"

His face lost the sparkle. "Has something happened?"

"A man died after being attacked outside the police station. These men were in the square around the time it happened, and the woman claimed to be the man's wife. Gage asked them to stick around, but you know they might decide to finish their vacation someplace else. The Sweet Spot is a popular coffee shop. I hope they'll keep coming back while they're here."

His nod was solemn. "So we can keep tabs on them." William could read through what I said, knowing there was much more to the story than I could share. "Take care, Lily—and you, too, Nikki. You two have a way of finding mischief."

I leaned over the counter and gave him a one-armed hug. I whispered in his ear that my witchy sense was in overdrive.

"Still, be careful."

"Always."

Nikki and I crossed the town square. She touched my arm. "What are you thinking?"

"This is crazy. Why would people try to pass themselves off as other people, especially a married couple, on vacation?"

"I'm sure you'll uncover that, but I am curious. That discount card you gave Tom Holden. Was there more to it than being nice?"

I slipped my arm through the crook of hers. "What makes you think I'd do something other than be kind?"

"I saw your lips move."

"Hm, maybe I should work on my ventriloquism. But you're right, I cast a quick spell so that if we should need to find the real Mr. and Mrs. Holden, we can."

"As long as they keep that card on them."

I grinned. "Who doesn't want to save money while they're on vacation? I'd think that was a nice incentive."

"You've become a little sneaky, my witchy friend."

"We use the skills we have, and sometimes, the spur of the moment is genius."

"Hopefully, your fiancé will feel the same way. Will you tell him what you did?"

"Absolutely, and I think he'll be impressed."

Nikki giggled nervously. "There are times when you overestimate what he finds impressive, especially in all likelihood he will tell you to stay out of the investigation."

I snorted. "Like that has ever worked."

Gage and Steve were leaning against his truck. As we approached, Gage said, "Did you learn anything new?"

Giving his lips a peck, I said, "Of course. The men were seen with our Jane Doe, and yesterday, she was in there with a different man matching our victim's description. William said if they come back, he will let us know."

Gage said, "Let me know, right, Lily?"

Nikki whispered, "Here it comes."

"Let us both know. Before you say that I need to stay out of this case, it's too late. I'm so far down the investigative trail you couldn't excise me with a wand."

"Not that I have one to use." He opened the passenger door for me. "Hop in."

I waved to Nikki. "See you at the house."

When Gage got in, he started the truck but waited for Steve to pull away from the curb first. "Is there anything you're not telling me?"

"No. But my thoughts are so jumbled I need my board to sort out the players, lies, and the truth. Oh, and have you heard from EL about the cash? As the real Simone said, there are no coincidences, and I have a gut feeling the satchel we pulled from the ocean today is connected. Especially since everyone seems to be focused on fishing. The real Tom, the fake Tom, the two Simones, and even our three wise guys from the town square.

"Funny you should ask. Right before you and Nikki got back, I got a text from EL. He's not positive, but he thinks the money is the work of a good forgery attempt.

I slumped against the seat, "And who said fishing and forgery don't go hand in hand?"

Chapter 8
Lily

I adjusted my clue board in the corner of the deck so it was in plain view of everyone. Gage started the charcoal for the grill, and Steve oversaw the project. Nikki and I had magically set the picnic tables so I could focus on the essential details and clues of the case. Milo stretched across the railing to see the clue board while Brutus and Murphy happily lounged in the grass, soaking up the sun. The rest of the group hadn't shown up yet.

In the center of the board, I had written:

Fake Tom Holden—deceased (Todd?) dressed
like real Tom
Bag of money
Fake Simone
Real Tom and Simone
Jetty rock
Felix Andrus
Eddie Capes
Wilbur Christy
Car door and tire squeal (red herring?)

Stepping back, I studied the meager list and tapped the marker to my lip. "What have I missed?"

"Who's Todd?" Nikki tapped the board.

"Jane Doe referred to the victim as Todd when Gage was questioning her. She said it was a pet name. For my money, that's his real name."

"Are we assuming the counterfeit money is connected to our mystery man's death?"

Gage said, "Don't jump to any wild conclusions."

"It's possible. How many times have you pulled a bag of money from the harbor, and there's been this much confusion right after?"

He shook his head. "Lily, remember, not everything has to be linked. But go with that theory for now, it's the most logical."

"That's my plan, but I'm wondering if I should wait for the gang to arrive before I spin out possible theories?"

Nikki said, "You won't have to wait long. I just heard a couple of motorcycles downshift."

Sharon and EL pulled their motorcycles close to the garage and shut them off. I didn't want to stare, but it was heart melting to see them have googly eyes for each other. EL pulled a bag from the saddlebag and they strolled hand in hand to the deck steps.

"Hello there. We brought corn on the cob from Marshalls Farm Stand." EL held it out for me. "It's ready for the pot, we shucked it there."

Sharon walked over to the clue board as EL took the corn in the kitchen. "This is a solid start, Lily. But where did the name 'Todd' come from? Oh, wait, I remember; Jane Doe used it in conversation about the victim."

Gage nodded at the board. "Lily thinks that's the man's real name."

EL joined us. "Are we ready to pick the clues apart?"

"Not until Mac gets here. I'd hate for him to miss out on the fun, and remember Margaret had some good ideas the last time we got together."

EL slipped his arm around Sharon's waist. "I have to say this is unconventional, working a case as a group."

Gage laughed. "You don't know the half of it. Lily's brain won't let it go until the pieces fit together like the perfect puzzle."

Milo grumbled, "That's what she does best."

I scooped Milo into my arms and whispered in his ear, "Be nice."

He glared at me. "Why? Nikki is the only person who can hear me, and she finds me utterly charming."

With a glance at my best friend, I noticed she was suppressing a laugh. "Nikki, would you help me in the kitchen? Please?"

The screen door slammed behind us, and I put Milo on the floor. "We should set out appetizers."

"My dear witch, did I upset you?" Milo growled softly.

"No, but I needed to clear my head, and we're supposed to be enjoying the day as a pre-wedding celebration. Now, I've set up a murder board on my back deck for my fiancé, fellow law enforcement folks, and friends to talk about instead of happy stuff."

Nikki wrapped her arms around me and held me tight. "There are two things I know about you. One, you love that man standing in front of the grill with every fiber of your soul and you're going to marry him in just over a month. Two, if we don't talk about what's happened, you won't be able to switch it off in your brain and enjoy the rest of the day." She looked me in the eye. "So, here's what we're going to do. Set a thirty-minute timer, and that's all the time we'll allow to discuss the case."

"Sixty." I smiled. "EL can talk a blue streak about technical stuff."

With a snap of her fingers, she had two trays overflowing with munchies. "Let's head back to the party and you can tell everyone the plan. This way, we'll still have a great time and take steps to solve the murder of Joe Doe."

"John Doe." I picked up a tray, and Nikki held the door for me.

"You say John and I'll say Joe, or maybe we should call him Todd." She winked. "After all, that's what the fake Mrs. called him."

I glanced over my shoulder and noticed Milo sitting in the middle of the floor. "Are you coming, Milo? The baby will be here soon and you find her fascinating."

"It's only because someone needs to keep an eye on her with those two big lugs in the middle of the lawn." He stalked out of the kitchen, his tail held high as it flicked from side to side. "A familiar was never to be a nanny, not even to your future children." He paused mid-step and turned to me.

I pointed to the backyard. "Go." That was interesting he thought there would be a child in the future.

Gage caught my eye and smiled. "Milo being his usual self?" He took the tray from me and set it on the table.

"You have no idea."

After settling baby Amanda on a blanket in the middle of the grass surrounded by Brutus, Murphy, and Milo, the adults enjoyed beverages and small plates of appetizers before I announced, "I have an idea." It sounded more like a proclamation.

"Today was supposed to be a celebration of our upcoming wedding." I smiled at Gage, who made a heart with his hands. "Unfortunately, we brought up a satchel of money, and a man died in front of the police station. With all of this happening, and we know I can't resist a puzzle of any kind," everyone chuckled. "Nikki made a brilliant suggestion. We'll discuss the case for *only* sixty minutes. Then I'll put the clue board in the house, and the rest of the day will be for fun only."

Margaret said, "Can you stop thinking about the case? From what little Mac said, it sounds fascinating."

"I can put it aside, but we all need to process what we saw and heard today and then, like good ribs, let it marinate until tomorrow."

Gage ran up the deck stairs, picked up my clue board, and brought it down to the seating area. He handed me the marker and asked, "Who's setting the timer?"

EL held up his phone. "On it."

I walked to the board and cleared my throat. Circling the bag of money, I tapped it. "How many of you think this murder is tied to the money?"

Mac said, "I have never believed in coincidence. There's a connection with the cash," he scanned the group. "Anyone else?"

EL said, "Forged money. I ran a couple of simple tests, and when one bill got wet, the green smudged. I did a little research. Some forgers use a specific green eyeshadow for patina but it's not waterproof."

"We'll need to get that confirmed with the Secret Service." Gage continued, "I'm hoping when we contact them tomorrow they'll take the money and not try to get involved in the murder case."

"Gage," I needed to point out the obvious, "If they're here, then the feds will stay involved." They'll need our help with the investigation, since we know the town and can get more information from our neighbors. Talking about the case now will clarify things for later."

Steve asked, "All right, so does anyone have a theory as to why our victim and Jane Doe would want to impersonate the real Mr. and Mrs. Holden?"

Sharon sipped her iced tea. "What if the actual couple's identity was so ordinary that the fake couple could do whatever they needed, like pass fake bills, and it would be blamed on the real Tom and Simone? We all heard the same story from Jane Doe about the argument for the fishing boat and getting seasick. It's a brilliant cover."

I paced in front of the board. "The genuine couple came to town for a quiet vacation, to do a little fishing, eat seafood, and unwind. The fake couple are here with the three men in the town park."

"How do you know that?" Margaret asked.

"Nikki and I went to the Sweet Spot before coming home. William mentioned he had seen Jane Doe and the three men together on several occasions, and Jill Dilly said she was with a blond man once."

She said, "It could have been vacationers exchanging tips about the area."

"It might have been, but William didn't think so, and neither do I. Remember, we're using the no-coincidence method for this case."

Mac leaned forward in his chair. "We're going to assume the five knew each other and *borrowed* the Holden's identity right down to the argument. Anyone at the B & B could have easily overheard that disagreement. How does that tie back to the money we found?"

"Both couples supposedly were going fishing. We went fishing, and we pulled up the bag. Could someone have placed the bag in a specific spot? Placing a tracker or something in it, so they'd know exactly where to go back and retrieve it?" I glanced at EL. "Did you find anything like that?"

"Like an AirTag?"

Nodding, I said, "Yes, that would give who-ever dumped the forged money a way to find it later."

"It's possible. I can check in the morning." His brow furrowed. "That's an excellent idea. We brought it up by accident, and the water that far out isn't over one hundred feet deep, so it's feasible."

I wrote waterproof *GPS tracking for a satchel* under Wilbur's name. "Now, was the rock found at the scene from a nearby jetty?"

Once again, EL was on the spot. "I'm still running tests, but that's my working hypothesis, and it was most likely the murder weapon, based on the traces of blood and size."

"Sweetheart, wrap up what you're thinking."

"What if," I paused, "Felix, Eddie, and Wilbur were working with the fake Holdens? They printed the forged money and needed to hide it for some unknown reason. Putting it in the waterproof bags and sinking the satchel with a GPS tracker for easy location later. But I don't see how the real Holdens fit into the equation—and why kill one of the gang?"

The group grew quiet as they thought about my ideas. "I just don't know why you'd need to involve an innocent couple. That makes no sense."

Sharon said, "It was a backup plan, like a second escape route. Divert the attention to someone else so you can get away with murder. Literally."

"Does that mean Jane Doe is a flight risk?" I glanced at Gage.

"Relax, Lily. For a change, I'm a step ahead of you. We located Jane Doe, and she's staying at the Coastal Motel. Officer Shepard is making sure she stays put. He'll bring her in for questioning if she's about to make a run for it. At this point, there's no reason for her or the men from the park to leave town. There's still the money to be retrieved, and they don't know that we found it."

Mac said, "That's if the money is why they were here in the first place."

These were excellent points. "We should alert the marina, Donnie White in particular, in case they want to rent a boat. With Donnie's business focused on lost treasure, it would be easy to convince him to take them out and that might put Donnie in danger."

Gage got up. "I'll call him now, and also, I'll get in touch with Nate to see who else might be a possible candidate for hire. Most of the local fishing charters want to go a few miles out. This group would look to hang close to shore."

"They might even try to rent a boat on their own. Ask Nate for Red Sweet's number. He's got a few boats he rents out for people who want to fish independently." I jotted that on the board next. Scanning the list of clues, I was feeling better. We had made decent progress.

"Sharon, we confirmed Simone's identity with her passport and license, but is it possible they were faked?"

"Anything's possible, but her license had that new REAL ID seal on it. Those are pretty hard to forge, but I'm not an expert. I'll run them through the DMV database and see what I find."

I added question marks next to their names. "Our last puzzle piece for today; who's Jane Doe." I noticed Gage was still on the phone, probably with Nate. "I'll call Monica at the motel and ask what name our suspect is registered under. She would have had to have given a credit card upon check-in."

Nikki said, "I'm going to the kitchen. Does anyone need something?"

EL stood. "I'll help."

They went inside, and I dialed the motel. Monica answered, "Good afternoon. Thank you for calling the Coastal Motel, Pembroke Cove's favorite motel near the beach. This is Monica."

"Monica, it's Lily. That's certainly a mouthful."

I smiled when she said, "It's marketing, Lily. I need every edge I can get on every reservation."

"I understand that. I'm sorry to bother you. I'm hoping you can answer a question or two."

"Anything for you. Do you have your sights set on a new puzzle of the concerning sort?"

"Unfortunately, I do. Can you tell me if a woman checked in earlier this week with short dark hair, average height, and weight? She might have been traveling alone or with a man."

"Yes. A couple checked in for an extended stay. He was blond, and maybe six feet tall, a little plump but not fat, and the woman was a brunette, of average height and weight."

"I'm pretty sure that's who I'm looking for. What name did they check in under, and did they provide a credit card?"

"Let me look."

I heard keys tapping, and she said, "I have it right here. Todd and Susan Fisher. They're booked for two weeks from this past Sunday, and they paid in advance for the full stay. The credit card I have on file, which was good by the way, was in his name."

"Thank you, Monica. As usual, will you let me know if you notice anything out of the ordinary?"

"You'll be the first, and I'll tell Torrie, too, since she covers the office more than I do."

"You're the best. We'll talk soon." When I put my phone aside, I wrote, "Todd and Susan Fisher" on the board next to Fake Tom Holden.

I turned to the group. "Who's going to research *the real* Susan and Todd Fisher?"

Chapter 9
Gage

Leave it to Lily to discover the identity of our mystery woman with one quick phone call. I didn't have the heart to tell her that Shepard already had that information and that the department was conducting a background check on them.

The sixty-minute timer gonged.

Nikki got up from the bench, took the marker from Lily's hand, picked up the board, and went inside. Everyone watching was stunned that she'd stop Lily mid-sleuthing. When Nikki came outside and closed the kitchen door with a firm tug, she said, "Who's ready to get murder off their minds and on a thick, juicy cheeseburger and fish?"

Lily looped her arm through Nikki's. "Is that your way of making sure we have fun today?"

"You agreed to one hour, and everyone's here to celebrate the upcoming nuptials of our dear friends. Not to solve a murder in one day, which isn't possible unless the perp walked in and gave themselves up."

I kept out of this conversation. Nikki was saying everything I wanted to say. I hated that our day had been derailed with a new case, but in police work, after we secured everything and there were no urgent matters, the case could wait until the morning, when we could attack it with fresh eyes and a rested brain.

Rubbing my hands together, I flipped open the grill cover. "Who wants a burger?"

.   .   .

Lily and I were sitting in an Adirondack chair for two with our legs outstretched in front of the fire pit. The last of our company had gone home. Milo rested on the arm of the chair and Brutus, who didn't like fire, lay on the deck. Stars dotted the inky night sky while fireflies danced at the edge of the herb garden. The night was almost perfect.

"Did you enjoy the barbeque?" I kissed the back of her hand.

"It was fun having everyone over, and once Nikki hid my clue board, it made it easier to relax and enjoy myself." She snuggled closer, and I wrapped my arm around her shoulders. "I was excited to show off Corbin's progress on the addition."

"Yeah. Mac said they're looking to add an extra bedroom to their place. They're talking about having another baby and need more room."

"Sharon and EL look good together."

"You were right to play matchmaker. He's a good guy, and now she's always got a smile on her face."

"Do you think he's right about the money being fake?"

And just like that, we were talking about the case. Not that I minded. If we didn't, Lily might not sleep tonight. "He's a bright guy, and before he moved to Pembroke Cove, he worked for a lab in Dallas. He's seen more than I ever hope to see. He also attended a seminar and sat in on one session about counterfeit money. If he says it's fake, then it is."

"Hm. Will the Secret Service take over the case or take the money and your report and leave town?"

"Are you referring to Todd Fisher's murder and our lengthy list of suspects?"

"Yes. Don't *you* want to be the detective to find out who killed him and why?" She emphasized the word "you" and I had to hide my grin.

"Of course I do. As a detective, I am driven to uncover the truth. With the feds coming to town, they'll want to know what we've discovered. But who knows? They might already have been tipped off about this specific forger and are working the case."

She sat up. "I'm going to the marina tomorrow and follow up on whatever Nate discovers about fishing charters or boat rentals. My money is on a private rental by the park lurkers. If Susan Fisher gets seasick, she might have stayed on land and let them drop the bag, but why hide it and get it later?" She slapped my leg. "Gage, we need to check with the bank and see if there's been an influx of one-hundred-dollar bills deposited from area stores. If there has been, are they the real deal?"

That was one avenue I hadn't thought of yet. "What do you think the chance of that is?"

"With all the visitors in town for the season? It's a safe bet we've got some floating around. I'm cautious when I accept them. I have a special ultraviolet light that can identify a forged bill. The bill's security thread shows, and each denomination is a different color. Fifties are yellow, and one hundred is pink."

That she checked bills coming into her

store didn't surprise me, but her level of detail about colors did. "And you've had no one attempt to pass a counterfeit bill?"

"Not yet, but if there are any circulating through the businesses in town, I want to know. Business owners deposit big bills. Now, if they're fifties, that's a different bubbling cauldron. Those could be used as change back to customers."

"Do me a favor. In the morning, let William know to keep an eye open for anyone who might try to pass a forged bill." I rubbed my hand over my five o'clock shadow. "I wonder if he has one of those lights?"

"If he doesn't, I'll give him one. Do you think we should alert other business owners?"

I had thought about that as we talked, but I didn't want to create a panic among the shopkeepers. "Not yet. The Sweet Spot is a good place for someone to try to exchange a large bill for a few sweets and coffee, so telling him is a good idea, and he'll keep it to himself. The restaurants are credit card-heavy with vacationers. But your store could be an excellent target to pass a large bill.”

“If someone comes in and tries, what should I do?”

“Get a message to me as quickly as possible. Chat the person up to stall them leaving, and when I arrive, I’ll handle the situation.”

She nodded. “That’s a good idea. I’ll have William do the same. We’ll have to alert Jill, too, since most mornings she’s on the cash register.”

I didn’t like that the circle of knowledge was already spreading, but Lily had a point about Jill. “Do you think she’d keep it quiet?”

“I do. She’s very loyal to William and knows he considers us family. It will be easy for her to keep it on the down low.” She pulled me up from the chair. “Care to do a walk-through of the addition and make some notes for Corbin? We’re running out of time to get every-thing wrapped up before we’re married.”

“What about the fire?”

“Leave that to me.” She held out her right

hand as Milo rose to a sitting position. His eyes were locked on Lily. "Flames that dance under the moon must die down soon. Now, it's time to transform into ash. For this I wish, so it shall be as I ask."

The flames died lower and lower to the ground as she held her hand level as if the fire pit were under it, until all that remained was a dark pile of ash. She gave a satisfied nod to Milo and took my hand.

"Shall we go inside?"

Milo purred, and she said, "Of course you're coming, too."

He ran up the steps, hopped over Brutus' back, and through his kitty door. My big lug was still snoring.

"Just leave him there. He's content."

The door eased open with a magical nudge from my favorite witch as we stepped over him. He snorted and rolled to the other side.

"We should leave it open in case he wakes up."

Milo purred again, and she wagged her

finger in his direction. "Be nice, Milo. In another month, we'll be living under the same roof."

He trotted off down the hall in the direction we were headed. As we walked, the lights came on, and I had to ask, "Did you cast a spell to have the lights turn on like a motion sensor?"

She grinned, "No. Corbin did that as a surprise for you."

The door to what was the larger part of the primary bedroom was ajar. "I asked Corbin to move the entrance to our room."

Windows overlooked the backyard, and a single glass door led to a new deck. Lily said, "I think we should put the bed against this wall so we can look outside and see the flower gardens when we wake up."

I opened a door that led into an oversized bathroom, and another door adjoined what was Lily's current bedroom. "Where does this go?"

"A new closet. I have a lot of clothes, and if you wanted to hang up a single shirt, there's zero room." She tucked her arm in mine. "I know it's bigger than we talked about, but I was thinking, if we ever had a little witch or non-magical, we'd want an extra bedroom so we can turn my current room into one."

My heart skipped. This was the first time she'd ever seriously mentioned having a child. "I know this is kind of late to the party, but kids?"

She nodded, and the twinkle in her eye spoke volumes. "Wouldn't it be fun if we had a couple? Nikki and Steve are talking about it, and Mac with his expanding family. If Sharon and EL stay the course, maybe we can have an entire classroom filled with our munchkins."

I pulled her into my arms and kissed her soundly. "I love how your mind works, whether it's talking about our future or solving a crime, it's just." At that moment, I was beyond happy and at a loss for words.

"Does this mean you like the idea?"

"I do. Now, what about the family room? Are we still expanding?"

"I think we're going to have to with all these

adults and kids running around." She placed her head on my chest.

After several long, bliss-filled minutes, she asked, "Gage, do you think someone chose the real Tom and Simone Holden randomly?"

"Let's have a cup of tea and look at your board. But to answer your question, I don't think it was by happenstance. Todd and Susan Fisher impersonated them, even down to his clothes. For the life of me I don't know why, other than the real Tom bears a striking resemblance to Todd Fisher."

We walked into the kitchen, and the teapot was already steaming. "How did you...?"

Her brow cocked. "I'm a witch." She looked up, and I knew that gleam in her eyes. "It's time we do a little digging, and before you say it's getting late and we've had a hectic day, I'm going to research anyway, so you might as well stick around. Two heads are better than one."

Milo yowled, and I jumped, not realizing he had entered the room. She picked him up and said, "He wants in on the research, too, and later, he'll prowl around town to see if he can run down any tidbits from his familiar network."

"That's a thing?"

She laughed. "Think of the familiars in town like extra eyes on the street. Milo always gets an interesting morsel or two."

I took Milo and held him out so that I could look him in the eyes. A low kitty grumble came from his chest. "Hold on there, little man. I want you to be extra careful when you're asking questions. How do we know all the familiars in town are on the right side of the law?"

He swiped a paw at me and grumbled again. Lily's hands covered her mouth, and she turned her back on us.

Milo yowled and wriggled his entire body. This time I got the message loud and clear. He wanted to be put down. I gently placed him on a kitchen chair.

"Gage, sweetheart. I love that you worry about Milo, but don't forget he was one of the most powerful witches in the Michaels family.

I'm sure he can see through a familiar that isn't true to the coven's code of ethics."

Milo glared at me but seemed to nod at the same time. He tipped his head and meowed to Lily.

"He says he appreciates your concern for his safety, but next time you want to talk to him, don't dangle him in mid-air like he was a baby with a stinky diaper."

"I'm sorry, old man."

He grumbled again and stalked out of the room, but Lily didn't translate this time. "What did I say?"

She put the teapot and cups on the table, pulled the board from the pantry closet, and then handed me a container of kitty treats. She pointed in the direction he had gone. "He doesn't like to be called old man. It makes him feel bad. Your best bet to get into his good graces would be to offer him some treats and a heartfelt apology."

"It's a term of endearment." I took the container and shook out an entire handful.

"Milo doesn't think so."

She was right, and I needed to apologize even if I couldn't understand his response. "Milo, come out for a second." When he didn't come into the kitchen, I walked down the hall. He sat near Lily's office door. His tail swiped the wooden floor in a jerky motion.

Kneeling, I placed a small pile of treats on the floor in front of him. He might nip me if I held them. "I'm sorry for calling you old. I never meant it as an insult but to point out the obvious: you *are* older than us."

He stared at me but didn't move to the treats.

"Can I call you little man?"

His tail stopped swishing, and he meowed before nibbling on a treat.

"I'm taking that as a yes." I ran my hand down his back and scratched under his chin. "Now, what do you say we help our favorite witch dissect more clues for this case?"

He ate the rest of the treats, bumped my knee with his head, and trotted to the kitchen.

Sometimes, a simple apology was the best way to reconcile differences.

Milo sat in a chair, and Lily was next to him. Her laptop was open, fingers poised on the keys. The clue board was in plain view of the table. Around the edges were photos she had taken today, and she was studying an image in her hand.

I pulled out a chair next to her. "Where to begin?"

Handing me the picture she had been studying, she asked, "Do you notice anything odd about this satchel?"

I looked closely at it and asked, "Do you have a magnifying glass?"

"I thought that would be your first question." She passed one to me. "Now, what do you see?"

"Very fine stitching on the base of the handles with the letters T and the beginning of an H."

She nodded. "Tom Holden."

Chapter 10
Lily

"I can't make out the brand on any of these images, but that's another thread we can tug after we look at it tomorrow. The tote is well-made and monogrammed, so it likely didn't come from a discount store."

Gage said, "This potentially ties our real couple to the money if the bag belongs to Tom Holden."

I paced. "If they're involved with the forgery, wouldn't it be logical they're also involved in the attack on Todd Fisher?"

"It would, but I need to speak with the

Holdens and show them a picture of the satchel. I'd like to see their reaction."

"Can I come with you? I want to witness that for myself."

He shook his head. "There are many ways I can give you free rein, but coming with me when I speak to a suspect isn't one of them. At least not this time, not with the Feds involved."

"Wait a sec. I've observed interviews at the station."

"True, but you can't ask your questions. I'm comfortable with you behind a one-way mirror." He held out his hand and pulled me into his lap. "It's late, and today has been a lot. What do you say we sleep on it and talk in the morning?"

"While you're questioning the happy couple, I'm going to the marina and chatting with Nate. We must learn where and when they rented a boat and dumped the bag. Another thought—why dump the money in the ocean unless the feds were closing in on them?"

"When EL confirms whether there's a

tracker in the bag, it would support the theory things were getting too hot to hang on to the counterfeit bills. It would make sense for the criminals to lie low in a small town like ours until things cooled down and then get back to laundering the bills."

I placed my hand on Gage's chest and gave him a light peck. "That makes total sense. So, here's how I see it playing out. The real Holdens set up Todd and Susan Fisher. The three men in the park became friendly with the Fishers when they arrived in town on vacation. At some point in the last few days, someone dropped the bag a ways offshore with the plan to retrieve it later. The only bad luck was we got it first."

"And Todd Fisher getting attacked?"

I shrugged. "He knew too much, and they killed him before he could talk." I snapped my fingers. "That's why he was near the station. He was coming to confess his part in the scam."

"Whatever the hoax is other than counter-feit cash."

Milo grumbled. "You're a little too trusting, my dear witch. Maybe they're all in on it together."

Gage tipped his head. "What does Milo think?"

"They're a gang of seven; whatever happened, they all did it."

"He might be on to something if the evidence supported it, but I think we have three separate groups. The men in the town square were observing the Fishers, who got caught up pretending to be people they're not, and the real Holdens are on vacation."

"But per the men, they all knew each other. I assumed they meant the Fishers and them, but somehow, Tom Holden's bag was at the bottom of the ocean." I shook my head. "I think somewhere between Milo's theory and yours lies the truth."

He yawned and squeezed his eyes shut, and then opened them.

"You're exhausted." I pulled him to a

standing position. "Time for you to head home and get some rest."

He wrapped his arms around me, resting his chin on my head. "Will you put this away for tonight?"

I yawned. "Yes. Fresh eyes and a rested brain are what I'll need to conquer tomorrow."

"That's what I thought earlier." Gage walked to the back door and called to Brutus. "Time to go home, boy."

The dog lifted his head, blinked a few times, walked into the kitchen, and melted onto the floor. I laughed. "Guess he's ready to stay the night."

"That's fine with me." He kissed me. "Sleep well."

I waited until he had backed out of the driveway before locking up. Then, using my cell I took a picture of the clue board and stashed it in the pantry. "Milo, time for bed."

"Lily, seriously, that big lug is staying over tonight. He can't even carry on a conversation with me and Murphy; all he wants to do is sleep."

I pointed to the bedroom door. "He's a non-magical familiar, and you like Gage, so Brutus is like you for him."

"That makes zero sense. You must be tired." He hopped on the bed and turned around three times before settling on his favorite pillow.

Brutus poked his head around the doorjamb and looked at me with the most mournful eyes. Milo lifted his head and groaned. "He is not sleeping on the bed."

"You can come in, Brutus." I knew Gage didn't let him sleep on the bed. Instead, I grabbed extra blankets from the linen closet, an oversized bed that Milo never used, and created a sleeping spot for Brutus in the corner where he could see us and still have plenty of space to stretch out. "Here you go." I patted the center of the blankets. He came over, turned around three times, and lay down.

"Milo, he might not be a familiar, but he's picked up on your turn and settle routine."

In a huff, he said, "I never said the big lug wasn't intelligent, just missing the magical touch."

I managed my bedtime routine, brushing my teeth and shutting off the lights with a flick of my wrist. I pulled the curtain back and stared at the crescent moon. I closed my eyes—for what reason, I didn't know—and I felt a surge of calming energy. Taking several slow, deep breaths, I closed the curtains, curled up next to Milo under the down comforter, and promptly fell asleep.

"What the?" I pulled myself from a deep sleep to discover not only Milo staring at me from his pillow but Brutus lying on the bed, his front paws crossed and ears perked. If dogs could grin, he was wearing one. I pushed myself to my elbow. "Good morning, fur-babies."

Milo shifted his head and glared at me. "Dogs aren't allowed on the bed."

"How would I know while I was sleeping he'd sneak up?"

"Really?" Milo stretched and swiped at Brutus. "Move, beastie."

"That's not nice." I scratched the top of the pup's head. "It's okay baby—Milo likes you."

He paused at the door. "Since you're awake, any chance for breakfast before noon?"

I glanced at the clock on the nightstand. "It's barely seven."

"You're wasting the best part of the day, you know."

He slunk out, and I tossed the covers back. "Brutus, are you hungry, too?"

A deep woof was all I heard before he leaped from the bed and went in the same direction as Milo. "Fur kids."

"I heard that."

I called out, "You were supposed to."

I dressed for comfort but nice for working at the bookstore. A floral skirt and short-sleeved sweater set with flat sandals. It would be warm today, and adding the sweater would keep me comfortable if the air conditioning got too cold.

My cell pinged. A text from Nikki.

Morning, what's the plan?
I replied, *Bookstore at nine?*

I got back a smile and coffee cup emoji. I filled the large bowl I had bought for Brutus with kibble, opened a can of tuna for Milo, and then poured myself a cup of steaming coffee.

"Thanks, Milo, for starting the pot."

He looked at the tuna I placed in front of him. "Thank you."

I gave him a side-eye. "No snarky comments as to why you're eating canned tuna?"

He glanced at Brutus. "He's eating kibble. I think compared to that abomination, my breakfast is delightful."

I heard a car door close and glanced out the back. Gage dashed up the steps and was at the door as soon as I opened it. He swept me into his arms and kissed me. "Good morning, beautiful. I thought I'd stop in for coffee and say hello to Brutus and Milo before we start our days."

"This is unexpected. I thought you'd be at the station early."

"I was, but the coffee's better here." He gave me a wink and poured himself a mug, adding a splash of cream and a spoonful of sugar. "Did the big lug behave last night?"

Milo glared at Gage. "He snores and kept me up."

Scratching the top of Milo's head, I said, "You didn't tell me that."

He ignored me but then grumbled, "You didn't ask."

"What's going on"? Gage ran his hand down the length of Milo's body, who moved his head in a small circle so that Gage could scratch everywhere possible.

"Milo said that he didn't get much sleep with the snoring."

He knelt next to Milo. "Don't worry, little

man, I'll get our favorite witch some strips for her nose to help her breathe."

I snapped a dishtowel at him. "Not me. Brutus."

"I know." He grinned, "Clue board in the closet?"

"It is. Breakfast?"

He arched a brow. "You want to cook?"

"Scrambled eggs and toast are easy. But if you'd rather take over, have at it." I got out the carton of eggs and a loaf of bread.

"You can do breakfast. If you don't mind, I'll add a few notes to the board."

I had cracked eggs into a bowl when I looked up after picking out the bits of shell. "Did you discover something? Did you see EL?" Now, he had my undivided attention, and the eggs were forgotten.

He smiled at me. "Since I've distracted you with information, I'll fix the eggs, then the details." He placed the skillet on the stove, took the whisk from my hand, and pointed to the loaf of bread. "You're on toast duty."

His firm tone told me he wouldn't share even the most minor tidbits until we had food on the table. "You're not going to make scribbles on the board?"

With a wide grin, he held up the whisk. "Right now, my sole focus is creating light *and* fluffy scrambled eggs."

"He's saying the same thing, light and fluffy, but it's funny how he's got your number." Milo yawned. "Might as well give it fifteen minutes, and he'll spill his guts. You know this is his style, to keep the suspect or, in your case, the nosy amateur sleuth waiting."

I scrunched my face and looked in Milo's direction. He could tell I wasn't thrilled but I said nothing since he was right. I'd have to be patient—however, it wasn't my best trait. I slid the slices of bread into the toaster. When I used magic, I leaned toward the burnt end of the spell. Using the non-magical gadget worked better.

"Nikki and I are planning to head to the

dressmaker in Drakes Bay soon for my final fitting."

"That should be fun, but I thought you had your mom's dress for the wedding?" He poured the egg mixture into the hot buttered pan.

"Mr. Grant altered and repaired some of the stitching on the dress for the ceremony, before he passed away. In addition, I wanted another dress for the beach reception, so I thought, why not? This is a very special day. His great-niece took over the shop and she made the second dress."

"That sounds like fun." He pushed the egg mixture around, and the toast popped up. "I'm just about ready."

"Me too." I buttered the toast, drizzled it with honey, and sat down.

Gage scooped eggs onto my plate and then his and took his time putting the pan in the sink.

"You know, my curiosity has gone into overdrive."

He took a seat, leaned over, and kissed me.

"Sweetheart, I don't want every second of our life to be talking about murders or other crimes in town. You're brilliant at solving puzzles, but for once, I'd like to start our day just being us, two people who can talk about something else besides murder."

My chin dipped. I had a terrible habit of getting tunnel vision when something happened around town. I placed my hand on his. "You're right, and I'm sorry." With a flick of my wrist, I turned the board around, so the brown backside faced us.

"I'll stop in and see Paige Reed at the library today. It's time we prepare for the fall movie season, and it'd be nice to have the first one after we return from our honeymoon. Besides, it's been a while since I checked in with her. I wanted to make sure she's gotten comfortable running the library."

"That's nice of you. She's had a bumpy start with her tenure and the amulet exhibit a few months ago." After Gage sipped his coffee, he said, "There was a GPS tracking device sewn into the satchel lining and those letters we thought we saw. It is definitely a T, and I'm sure the second letter is an H."

I tapped the table. "I knew it. So, the fishing trip had to be a ruse to look for the money." I flipped the board to face us with a snap of my fingers. "Which couple, the real or fake, are the ones who were going to charter the boat? And how will I get anyone to identify them positively?"

"We've pulled the DMV files on the two couples. I could send you the information if you promise to be careful."

I couldn't help it, a grin filled my face. "That would be a tremendous help. Nikki's meeting me at the bookstore at nine, and we'll get started. The first stop is the marina. Like I said, I want to see William and a few other shop owners next. I'm not asking everyone if they've been passed bad bills, it'll be a casual conversation about business. I'll have Aunt Mimi cover the store for a few hours as we make our rounds. What will you do about the bank since

I can't go in there and ask questions about the phony bills?"

"When I leave here, I'm headed back to the station, calling the bank to get an appointment with Chuck Yancy. He's the new VP over at the bank."

"Want to meet at the shop for lunch, around twelve? I'll pick up sandwiches, which gives me an excuse to run into Robin's Café and chat with Regan."

"Sounds good. Get enough for Sharon and Mac, too. We can have an informal debrief after we've all had time to follow up on leads."

"Aunt Mimi will still be there in case I have to run out in the afternoon."

Milo grumbled. "If the two of you are done making plans, can I get a saucer of kitty milk?"

I pointed to my lap. "Is that your way of asking for attention? Come here, you little fur ball."

He leaped into my lap and purred loudly. "Can I get a treat at lunch, too, since I'm going to help Mimi watch the store?"

Laughing, I said, "Yes. Everyone will have lunch, including you."

Gage scratched under his chin. "Milo, are you going with Lily today?"

His purring stopped, and he gave Gage a solemn nod. "Now that Detective Cutie mentioned it, I must go with you. There could be some highly compassionate person at the dock who'll take pity on this poor cat and toss me a fish."

I laughed, "Milo, why do you always think of your belly first?"

"Practice makes for perfection, my dear witch, and maybe you should read a little in your book before we start sleuthing today."

That's something he hadn't said for a while. "Maybe I will."

Chapter 11
Lily

My book, *Practical Beginnings*, lay open on the counter at the store. Over the last year, I realized every time I was involved with a crime, the book would show me a spell that might come in handy. Currently, the pages in the book were blank until I turned to the next one. I smiled. Now, this might be useful. A long-distance eavesdropping spell.

"Milo?"

When he didn't answer, I went searching for him. He wasn't in the kiddie corner or the window seat taking a sunbath. "Milo, are you hiding?"

By chance, I looked out the front window, and Milo was trotting next to Nikki as she approached the front door with coffee and a pastry bag. Some things we could always count on.

I stood in the open doorway and took the bag when she reached me. "Good morning."

"Look who I found out wandering?" She gestured to Milo, who was already reclining in the window seat.

"That's where you went. Were you out looking for clues?"

In a deep kitty growl, he said, "Of course. I checked on the five suspects staying at the B & B, which're all accounted for. Mabel needs to hire a better housekeeper. There's a lot of dust bunnies under the furniture."

"Noted, but did you learn anything new?"

"The happy couple eats in silence. He reads the newspaper and she has her nose in a book, which today's tome ironically is titled, *Counterfeit: A Novel*."

I crossed my arms over my chest. "Now that's interesting."

Nikki said, "I haven't read the book. Is it about counterfeiting money?"

"No. It's about two college friends who are involved in fake designer handbags. But it's curious that Simone would read anything of that nature."

"Do you think that means they're the people behind the scheme?"

"Nikki, that's the question of the hour. As soon as Aunt Mimi gets here, we're going to buzz over to the B & B, then stop in to see William, and we'll meet Nate at the marina. We need to see men about boat rentals."

"What do you think we'll learn when we run by the inn?"

"I'm hoping we bump into Wilbur Christy. He was the one that pointed a finger at Susan Fisher." I flipped open my laptop. "We never dug into the Fisher's background. It's time we do."

Milo trotted to the counter, crouched and did a quick spring off his back legs, landing next to the computer. "You don't have a lot to go on with them."

"No, but didn't she say something about Boston?" I looked at Nikki, the wheels in my brain turning. "That was Wilbur. He said they all live in the Boston area, within several miles of each other."

"Was he talking about Susan and Todd or the two other men?"

"We're going to track them all down."

She took the lid off a cup and handed it to me. The subtle aroma of vanilla teased my senses. I opened the bakery bag and pulled out an over-sized blueberry muffin, causing my taste buds to weep. "This will hit the spot." I sighed and looked in her direction. "If my dress is too tight on my wedding day, can we magically let it out?"

"First off, you won't need to worry about

that, but with magic we can accomplish almost anything."

I took a bite and the blueberry flavor burst in my mouth; the glaze was a tart lemon. "There's nothing like muffins made with seasonal berries." When I looked at the screen, Todd and Susan Fisher were listed to the same street address. I jotted down the information and then moved on to Tom and Simone Holden. Within seconds, the results came up empty for Boston. That was strange. I couldn't recall where she had said they were from.

Next, I typed in each man's name and they all came up as Wilbur had said, close in proximity and less than ten miles from the Fishers. Close enough.

Nikki peered over my shoulder as I jotted down notes. "Well, that confirms they could have known each other in Boston, or at least crossed paths."

I added the home address of each suspect to my pad. "Now, we need to widen our search for the Holdens." Typing in their names to the search bar, a list of addresses came up, but no social media accounts, either professional or personal. If the search results were accurate, they moved to a new city every year. Why would anyone do that? Moving takes so much effort.

"Look at this." I turned the screen so Nikki could see it. "What's your take?"

"Nobody moves that much. You'd never get unpacked and settled."

I turned the screen back to face me. "That's what I thought. Maybe they move for their jobs."

With a snort, she said, "Criminals might travel light?"

"Living in furnished rental homes would make it possible. Pack a few suitcases and a couple of boxes of personal items and toss them in the back of a large SUV. You're hitting the road for a new adventure."

It sounded good in theory. Why would anyone want to live a vagabond life, never putting down roots? But it took all kinds to make the world go around.

The door to the shop burst open. Aunt Mimi came in with a *whoosh*. "We're here." She had an oversize tote hanging off her arm and Phoenix, her familiar, slunk in after her. "Lily, dear. Nate wanted me to tell you he'll meet you near his boat slip. He thinks it would be better, and I do as well, that you don't talk to anyone who rents boats alone."

She held up her hand to silence me. "Not that he doesn't believe you can't handle yourself. We all know that you're a formidable sleuth and witch, but sometimes these old codgers tend to talk more freely to a man."

As much as I hated the statement, and I know she did, too, she was right. "That's fine, Aunt Mimi. Whatever gets us the results we need. That's what counts."

She held out the tote. "Will you put our lunch in the refrigerator? Before you ask, there is plenty for half the police force. I figured

Gage, Mac, and Sharon would join us for lunch. Maybe even that cute doctor, EL?"

I kissed her cheek. "What are you now, a fortune teller?"

She smiled but didn't answer the playful question. "Why don't you ladies grab your magnifying glasses and do what you love to do? Follow the clues. Phoenix and I will take care of the store. It's just like old times."

Nikki gave her a quick hug, took the tote bag, and magicked it into the refrigerator. "Mimi, you're the superstar. Bringing lunch for us. Can we get you something when we come back?"

I nodded. "We'll get beverages."

Aunt Mimi pulled knitting needles and yarn from her purse. It didn't look big enough to hold that type of project but the bag belonged to a witch, so anything was possible.

"I packed dessert, too." She waved her wand, and my coffee cup hovered in midair directly in front of me. "Don't forget your coffee, Lily."

"Thank you." The door opened of its own volition. "I guess we're leaving. Come on, Milo." He trotted after us as we reached the sidewalk. The door closed firmly.

"Do you think she wanted to get rid of us?" I glanced over my shoulder. She was talking to Phoenix and knitting.

"Phoenix told me, in confidence, I might add, that Mimi gets a kick out of you sleuthing with Nikki, which is why she's always thrilled to run the shop in your absence." Milo took a sharp right, and we followed.

My steps slowed at the bottom of the stairs leading to the alley. Raised voices drew my attention to the left side of the inn. "Nikki, over here."

I quickened my pace and put a hand out to stop her forward motion. I stuck my head around the corner. Tom Holden stood in the middle of Wilbur, Eddie, and Felix.

"Who's the stupid idiot responsible for the feds showing up?" Tom looked at each man, his nostrils flaring. "Killing Todd was right out of the handbook about what not to do."

Wilbur nudged Eddie, who in turn, jabbed Felix.

"Do you have something to say for your-selves?" Cracking his knuckles, he paced in front of the men.

Eddie said, "Tom, we didn't"

Tom jerked his hand across his throat. "I don't want to hear your justification. Simone had to find an excuse to talk with Susan. You know those two don't get along. Don't worry; we'll clean up this mess and get back to business."

"We still need to charter the fishing boat." Wilbur said, grabbing Eddie's arm, his finger-tips pressed into the flesh, making deep white impressions.

Tom stopped pacing. "For what?"

Felix chimed in, "It's what people do on vacation. Go fishing."

"Ha. It's easier to go to the market and buy

a pound of filets or find someone who sells it at the dock. Don't waste your time."

Nikki tugged on my skirt. I didn't move, not yet. I wasn't ready to miss out on a potential, or substantial lead.

Eddie nodded to Wilbur and Felix. "Maybe you should come with us for the day. You might find it enlightening."

"I have a wife to keep happy. Besides, there's still Susan to deal with and, since the three of you aren't confessing to trying to knock some sense into Todd's head, I'm going to have to work on her."

"We might be a lot of things—slackers has been your favorite word to describe us—but you need to be careful how you talk to us, Tom. We're just the tip of the tsunami."

Tom narrowed his eyes. "Is that a threat, Wilbur?"

"Not at all. Remember, when you joined this project, you knew we reported to others."

"I figured you weren't the brains of the outfit. Maybe once this mess dies down, it might be a good time to meet them. You know, let them see the value I bring to the table."

Eddie shook his head. "You haven't even been around six months. There's no way anyone's gonna want to have a sit down with you."

Milo wound around my legs. When I reached to pick him up, he slipped between my hands, walked a few steps, and then paused. I tipped my head, wondering what he needed.

Nikki tugged again on my skirt and bobbed her head in Milo's direction. I moved away from the side of the building and hurried after them. When there was a decent distance between us, I asked, "What's wrong?"

Milo's attention was behind me. When I looked back, Tom was striding in the opposite direction. Strangely, he was heading straight to the police station.

He growled, "Go inside the inn, now."

I followed him and Nikki up the steps. We had just entered the lobby when Simone came from the parlor. She stopped in her tracks when she saw us.

"Hello. This is a surprise." Then she forced a weak smile. "Cute kitty." She bent over and extended her hand.

Milo played his part as a typical feline, sniffed her, and then allowed her to scratch the top of his head, where he rewarded her with a purr. I could hear it now that he would need smoked salmon after this excursion.

"That's Milo. He's a rescue."

He glared at me, and I smiled. "We've been together for quite some time."

"He's beautiful."

With a grumble, he said, "Handsome. The word is handsome." He strolled away just far enough to prove his point that he wasn't an ordinary cat.

"What are you ladies doing here this morning?"

I stepped closer. "After the shock you had yesterday, we wanted to check on you and make sure your husband, Tom, is well."

"We're both fine. I guess it's true what

we've heard about small towns. Everyone's very friendly."

"We try," Nikki said. "Do you have plans today?"

She twirled her long necklace around her index finger. "We might visit a friend who's vacationing in the area. Tom's talked about going fishing, but I'd prefer the beach. Is there someplace we can get a picnic to take with us?"

I smiled at Nikki. "Robin's Café has wonderful picnic fare. They can even put it in a small cooler if you plan on taking a boat out."

"Tom would love that. To putter around with the waves lapping against the hull. It sounds nice."

"Don't you get seasick?" My voice was full of sweetness as I smiled at her.

"Oh, Tom got me those pressure bands to wear on my wrists and even something that goes behind the ear. He swears that the motion of the ocean won't bother me at all." She grinned. "I made a rhyme."

"Well, if you decide to take a boat, remember to wear a life jacket and cruise out past the point. We have an old lighthouse that is spectacular when viewed from the water."

"Lily, that's good to know." She nodded toward the stairs. "I should get ready. Tom will be back soon. He stepped out to get," she looked around the room, "the newspaper. He enjoys reading it every day."

"It's good to keep up on current events," Nikki said. "Enjoy the rest of your day."

"You, too, and thank you for checking on us. We've both recovered nicely from our scare yesterday. It's moments like that that should be a reminder to us all to treasure those we love. I decided to stop arguing about doing something that makes him happy."

"Like going fishing?" I quipped.

Through gritted teeth, she said, "Exactly."

The smile was so forced I thought her cheeks would crack from the strain. "Nikki, we should get going. Simone needs to get ready for a day on the water. Don't forget a hat and sunscreen."

Her face relaxed. "An excellent reminder. Thank you again, Lily. You've been so kind, and when we get back, I'd love to stop by your bookstore. I'm an avid reader. Maybe you could pick something out for me?"

"Do you have a favorite genre?"

"I'll read anything between covers, even cookbooks."

"I'll make a few selections, and you can take your pick. What time do you think you'll stop in?"

"You close at four?"

I hid my surprise that she knew the store hours. "That's right."

"Then I expect it will be three-thirty."

I gave her my best bookstore owner smile. "I'll wait for you."

Chapter 12
Gage

I sat in the hard, wooden chair, waiting for Chuck Yancy. We were supposed to have been meeting fifteen minutes ago. Drumming my fingertips on the arm in a steady rhythm, I watched the seconds on the clock tick off. It reminded me of an interrogation room clock. Weren't banks supposed to be a friendly place?

"Detective Erikson. I'm sorry to have kept you waiting."

A young guy, barely thirty, crew cut, chiseled

jaw and pale blue eyes, bustled into the room. A pale, lavender pocket square, which matched his paisley tie, accessorized his light gray tailored suit. He stuck his hand out and gave mine a vigorous shake. "Always good to become acquainted with local law enforcement, but I sincerely hope I never need your official services." He pulled out his high back, leather desk chair and sat down.

"Don't worry. I'm not here because something is wrong, necessarily, but we need to talk about a serious and potential issue." I watched as his face fell.

His desk phone rang, but he ignored it. "You have my undivided attention."

To his credit, he continued to focus on me. "Recently, a cache of counterfeit one-hundred-dollar bills was discovered locally. I can't give you specifics on where or how, as this is an ongoing investigation, but are you aware of any instances where a counterfeit bill was presented over the counter or in a deposit from one of the local shop owners?"

"No. I did not expect to hear this kind of news in a sleepy little town."

I wanted to laugh and tell him Pembroke Cove was anything but sleepy, but I'd let him find that out for himself. I didn't ask again but waited for him to process his thoughts.

"If one of the tellers had seen a fake bill, I would have been among the first to know. But now that I'm aware of the situation, I'll reach out to you immediately if we do. How do you plan to handle it with the businesses? Will you tell them or wait?"

"The Secret Service will be here this morning. I intend to ask them what they recommend my best course of action be. I don't want to alarm everyone, but I believe the authorities know this particular person or persons who are printing the money. I'm sure, like all criminals, they have a signature style."

His head bobbed. "Good point. Relying on them will be the right approach."

I stood and extended my hand. "Welcome

to town, Chuck. And here's my card. If you need to reach me, don't hesitate."

"Thank you for stopping in. I'll talk with the tellers but ask them to keep it quiet outside of the bank."

"I'd appreciate that."

Once outdoors, I noticed the humidity was rising. My thoughts drifted to Lily, and I wondered how she was making out by following the clues she thought were important. Especially the boat angle.

A reminder tone went off on my cell and I hurried to my sedan. The agents would arrive in the next thirty minutes. I'd rather be sitting at my desk than just walking into the station when they arrived.

I sent a brief text to Peabody and Mac. *Meet me in my office at ten.*

I parked in the back lot and entered through the employee-only door. The station was unusually quiet. The break room was empty, so I poured myself a mug of coffee. I wasn't sure how to best prepare for this meeting. This was the first time I had dealt with counterfeit money. I made my way down the hall, glancing into the empty interrogation rooms. I had a clear view of the front desk when I reached my office. Alice was speaking with two women dressed in dark suits. I set my mug aside and hurried out front; so much for a thirty-minute window.

"Alice?"

Her face flushed as she said, "Detective Erikson." The tremor in her voice betrayed her nerves. "These women are here to see you."

The taller of the two extended her hand. "I'm Agent Flores and this is Agent Peters."

The other agent did the same. "Althea Peters. You're friends with my cousin Dax." She gave me a warm smile.

I wondered if she was a witch. Dax Peters came from a long line of witches and never mentioned any of his siblings or cousins were non-magical, so I was going to assume she was.

I shook their hands. "It's a pleasure to meet

you both. Agent Peters, Dax never told me his cousin was in a similar line of work."

"Gage, I've heard so much about you that I feel like we're family. Call me Althea. And my cousin and I share all our talents." She confirmed her witchiness with a wink, and her soft southern accent reminded me of Dax's.

Agent Flores said, "Nola. Unless we're in front of a suspect."

"Noted. I'm Gage." I gestured to my office. "Coffee?"

"Please." I wasn't sure which agent agreed, since now their voices had the same monotone timber.

"I'll let Detectives Peabody and Sullivan know to meet in your office." As an afterthought, Alice said, "And I'll bring coffee."

"Thank you, Alice."

Althea took the chair closest to the window and Nola settled into the first one. She said, "Thank you for calling us. We're certain this is a fringe group broken off from a larger contingent printing money."

"How can you be sure?" I settled into my chair, wondering where my team was. The agents had me at a disadvantage.

Althea said, "Your lab technician sent us high-resolution images."

I coughed. "EL is the coroner. Dr. Edgar L. Dawson. But he's an expert resource when it comes to many things."

Nola's brow quirked. "Including forgery? We want to interview him. I'm sure that can be arranged?"

I heard the question in her response. She was a stickler for maintaining the image of a hard-driving agent. "Certainly."

She gave a brisk nod. "Please ask him to transport the money, too—and with a police escort. These criminals would do anything to get the evidence out of your custody."

"Agent Flores, we have not made the discovery public."

"That might be, however, never underestimate the professional criminal mind." She crossed her legs as she leaned back in the chair.

"If you will excuse me for a moment, I'll arrange for a detective to accompany him." I nodded to Althea and left the room.

Peabody and Mac were walking toward me, carrying mugs of coffee. "Hey, boss, Alice asked us to bring in coffee."

"Thanks, Mac. Our guests would like a cup but don't want to engage in pleasantries."

"All right." He looked at Peabody. "We should run down a few leads."

I took the mugs of coffee from him. "Not yet. Who wants to pick up EL and the satchel and come back here? Agent Flores has requested his presence and said we shouldn't underestimate the criminal mind, so EL must have an escort."

Peabody said, "We'll go. They should appreciate double the protection."

"Thanks, oh, and in an interesting twist, Dax's cousin is Agent Althea Peters. She's sitting in my office with Agent Flores."

Peabody's eyes widened. "Did you know he had a cousin in the business?"

"I didn't. You better hurry. I'm sure Nola Flores is eager to see the satchel's contents and interrogate EL."

Mac said to her, "I'll drive, and you can let him know we're on the way."

"Great, and if he has anything new on Todd Fisher, ask him to be prepared to share that information as well."

"You got it, boss." Mac followed Peabody out the back and I took the coffee to the women.

"It's hot." I handed the mugs to Althea and Nola. "The detectives should be back in about twenty minutes with Dr. Dawson."

Althea smiled. "Thank you. Now tell us everything you can about the satchel."

"My fiancée, Lily, and friends—including two detectives, Dr. Dawson, and three civilians —went fishing early yesterday. While anchored about two hundred yards offshore, Margaret, Detective Sullivan's wife, cast her fishing line. It wasn't long before she thought she hooked a fish. Upon reeling it in, we discovered the satchel, and inside were stacks of money stored in Ziploc bags with a purple tab."

I gave them each an apologetic smile. "The devil is in the details. If I over-explain, ask me to keep moving."

Nola held up her hand. "Details are critical, and you'll have no complaints from us."

Althea nodded. "Please, continue."

"We came to shore immediately since I wanted to secure the money. While at the station, I did a cursory check for a bank robbery, but nothing popped. Shortly after we returned, a man was attacked in front of the police station. By the time we got to him, he had expired."

Althea leaned forward. "Do you know the identity of the man?"

"Not at first. We originally identified him as Tom Holden but later determined he was Todd Fisher."

They both looked at each other and shifted in their chairs.

"Do those names mean something to you?"

Nola said, "They've come up in our investigation. Was anyone else involved?"

"The woman who initially said he was Tom had pretended to be Simone Holden. But later, we identified her as Susan Fisher, and three men were witnesses in the town square."

Althea leaned forward. "And they are?"

"Felix Andrus, Eddie Capes, and Wilbur Christy." It was easy to see by the twitch at the corner of Nola's eye that she was familiar with those names.

She asked, "Any idea where these people currently are?"

"The Holdens and the men are staying at the Pembroke Cliffs Bed & Breakfast. I've asked them to stay in town for a few days in case I have more questions. Susan Fisher has a room at the Coastal Motel and she's currently under surveillance by one of my officers."

"You should have them all under surveillance." Nola's voice was sharp. "Do they know about the satchel?"

"Not to my knowledge. It's not like we put

an article in the morning edition of the Pembroke Edge."

"So other than the people on the boat when you recovered the satchel, no one else knows?" Nola continued, "And all these people are trustworthy?"

"I'd trust all of them with the combination to Fort Knox. In fact, they all worked together and rescued me after I had been kidnapped a short time ago. They're as dependable and loyal as a Bernese Mountain dog."

"Are they as fierce?"

"Agent Flores, I give you my word they will never share anything like gossip." I was sure using her title got my point across.

"You understand, with an ongoing investigation such as this, we try to keep everything close to the vest."

"I've been in law enforcement for fifteen years, and I might work in a small town, but we've had our share of crime. Confidentiality is always a top priority."

My cell buzzed and I glanced at the screen.

"They're back. We should move into a conference room." When I stood, they did as well. "Follow me."

We walked down the hall into the large room that faced the back. The eyebrow windows provided natural light, but no one could see inside. The agents took seats with their backs to the wall.

Peabody and EL entered first. He was carrying the satchel in an evidence bag. Mac closed the door once he was inside.

I made introductions before my team sat.

EL said, "Agent Peters, you bear a strong resemblance to your cousin."

"Everyone says that." She smiled and gestured to the satchel. "Is that the bag that was recovered from the Atlantic?"

He placed it in the center. "Yes. I've discovered a few things in the last twenty-four hours. The first is that there are initials near the handle, T.H. In addition, a GPS tracker was placed in the bag's lining. The logical assumption is whoever dropped it intended to go back for it."

"Agreed." Nola glanced at Althea. "How did you discover the money was counterfeit?"

"I ran a UV light over it, and the telltale strip was missing, but prior to that, the green ink smudged. I attended a conference several months back on the topic of inks used by forgers. One trick was a particular green eyeshadow."

Althea asked for gloves. Mac handed her and Nola a pair.

"If you don't mind, I'd like to open the bag?" She looked at Nola, who nodded.

"It's your case now." I felt it was important to show that we were being totally cooperative.

They carefully examined every aspect of the money, the knife, and the gun, putting everything back in the evidence bag before they spoke to us. "Are there documents we need to sign so you can release this to us?"

I said, "Alice will prepare them."

"Good." Nola gave a brisk nod. "Now, about the murder victim. You believe it's Todd Fisher?"

"Yes." EL said, "A blow to his temple with a rock caused his death."

"No witnesses?" Althea asked.

"None that have provided solid evidence. Wilbur Christy pointed the finger at Susan Fisher. The other two said they heard a car door slam and tires squeal but didn't see the victim get out of a vehicle or be thrown out. In addition, we have no visual evidence on our security cameras there was a car. However, Mrs. Fisher identified him as Tom Holden. It was chaotic in the beginning."

"And now?" Nola said.

"We're investigating and following up on several leads. The most important is who chartered a boat and could have dropped the bag into the ocean at some point in the last few days. We believe the two incidents are linked but unsure how."

Althea said, "Excellent."

"We were able to get prints from Andrus but not the other two. Capes touched nothing, and Christy took his water bottle with him.

However, he said that no one was going to pin this murder on him." I leaned on the table. "That's a curious statement, don't you think?"

The agents remained silent. But I could outlast almost anyone at that game.

Nola finally dropped her shoulders and nodded to Althea. She said, "They're minor associates of a crime family. They've each done a stint in jail at different times, but nothing serious. Low-level crimes."

"Do you think they're behind the counterfeit scheme?" I wanted to ask why they hadn't led with that information, but it wouldn't change anything that we knew now.

"They're too far down the chain of command. They know someone who knew someone else, it's that kind of a game. We've been watching them, hoping they'd lead us to the main person making the major decisions, but so far it's been a dead end."

Peabody asked, "Has something changed?"

The agents didn't answer her question. Althea said, "Dr. Dawson, could we see the victim? We may be able to confirm his identity."

EL never blinked, even if he thought it was unusual. It confirmed my suspicion: their jurisdiction didn't cover murder unless it was directly tied to the money.

I pushed back my chair. "Why don't we all go?"

Chapter 13
Lily

Milo had informed us that after our stop at the B & B, he was returning to the bookstore to get out of the hot sun. As Aunt Mimi said, Nate was waiting for us at his boat slip. He was smiling from ear to ear.

"I was glad to hear you needed my help today." He lowered his voice and slung his arm around my shoulder. "Lily, I've been down here just monitoring things, and it's been pretty quiet. No one is looking to rent or charter a boat today, at least in person. They could have made arrangements by calling or emailing, of course."

"If my hunch is correct, Tom Holden will try to rent a boat later this morning. Do you think Red Sweet would contact me if someone tries to rent one of his?"

"He's a decent fella, no reason to believe he won't. Especially if he thinks folks are up to no good."

"We should talk to him first and then Donnie White unless you think otherwise?"

"Donnie first; he's waiting for his customers right now. They're running late." He steered us in the direction of where *Donnie's Treasure* was moored. He grinned, "I'll let you do all the talking and be your muscle if you need it."

I didn't need to remind him that Nikki and I could disarm a couple of fishermen if we were in danger, but I appreciated the sentiment. Our sandals clomped over the wooden planks as we drew closer to the slip. Donnie stood on the boat's bow and nodded at me as I lifted my hand in greeting. He hung his head, and I could see his mouth moving. I wasn't his favorite person after what had transpired during Nikki's wedding at the B & B.

"Hi, Donnie." We stayed on the dock.

He made his way down the boat's length and hopped down beside me. He nodded to Nate and looked at me. "What can I do for you? Looking to charter the boat for an excursion?"

"Not today, but glad to hear you'd take us out."

"Lily, I've got no beef with you. I'm embarrassed by what happened in March."

I remembered what Milo had said about the dust bunnies, and the inn had an excellent reputation. I wanted to help. "Mabel seems to be doing well at the inn. It's a lot for one person to handle. If you need additional housekeeping help, I could let you know if I hear of anyone looking for work."

"Appreciate that. Now, you didn't come down here to talk about the inn. What do you need?"

I pulled out my cell phone with the pictures of my suspects. "Can you look at these people and tell me if any of them charted your boat in the last week? Maybe a little before that, but not much."

He took my phone and scanned the images. After glancing my way and then back at the screen, he handed it back. "All but two are staying at the inn, but no one has chartered the boat, which is too bad. Business has been slow this season."

"You're sure? They might have wanted to fish and not dive."

Shaking his head, he turned to his crew. "Men, anyone asking around about a fishing charter or boat rental?"

Keith Hansen, one of his crew members organizing the air tanks, looked our way. "Yeah, I saw a couple of people at Betty's Market looking at the community board. They were talking about a boat rental." He took his cap off and rubbed his forehead. "Must have been last Thursday, maybe Friday. I mentioned I worked for a charter, but they wanted to take the boat out themselves. I mentioned Red and gave them the slip number." He gave me a long look, which was hard to read. "If you're asking, I'm guessing they're up to no good."

"Possibly, and thanks, Keith, for the information."

He put his hat on and went back to his task. Donnie stuck his hands in his pockets. "I'm guessing if anyone comes around, you'd like me to let you know?"

"I'd appreciate it—or call Gage."

"Consider it done." He climbed aboard his boat and left us standing on the dock.

Nate said, "Next stop, Red's slip."

Nikki glanced back at *Donnie's Treasure.* "I'm surprised Keith gave you any information since he was a top suspect in the death of John Bailey."

"He was cleared." I wasn't defending myself, just stating a fact.

"Lily, those guys hold a grudge even if they

discovered how their actions created doubt about their morals and ethics. I think until St. Patrick's Day, they thought they could treat anyone however they wanted, with no consequences."

I didn't want to dwell on the past and was glad something good came from John's death. "Hopefully, Red will have some good news on a rental." I tried to lighten my voice, but we all knew what was at stake. Solving the murder of Todd Fisher, even if he was the bad guy in all of this.

"Nikki, put yourself in Susan Fisher's shoes, and I'm making a few assumptions. Todd Fisher had the satchel. Either he stole the bag from Tom Holden or deliberately had something monogrammed to throw suspicion off himself. If you were Susan, would you know what your husband had been doing? Don't answer too quickly. Remember, there was the borrowed argument from Simone, who gets seasick. And after this morning, we know they all know each other."

Her steps slowed. "Don't you think this entire situation is confusing? We have two couples claiming to be the real Tom and Simone Holden; only one has the right identification. The other is Todd and Susan Fisher. The three men and Mabel are reporting that the couple had an argument, and there's a satchel of counterfeit bills, and one man is dead. How do the three stooges from the town square play into all of this?"

"I agree with you if we take it all at face value. We know Tom and Simone are the couple staying at the inn. We also know at some point, while they've all been in town, they've crossed paths with the others but are pretending they don't know each other. One couple had to rent a boat and drop the bag into the ocean to be retrieved later. It's our mission to find out which of our suspects rented the boat. Once we figure out that piece of the puzzle, we should have a clearer picture of who's responsible for what."

Nate chuckled. "That's as clear as the bottom of the ocean during a storm."

"I know." We walked down the gangway. At the end was Red's charter business. I tapped on the side of the fiberglass boat and called out, "Hello."

Red Sweet popped up from behind the other side. "Hi, Lily, Nate, and is that you, Nikki?"

"Yes, it's me," she waved.

Red scurried over the gunwale and jumped to the dock. "How can I help you today? Looking to charter a boat for something? But I heard Gage's new boat is the bomb."

"We're hoping you can give us some information about a few people who might have rented a boat from you in the last week or maybe even ten days." I withdrew my cell and pulled up the images. "Do any of these people look familiar?"

He scrolled from right to left. "I sure did."

"Which ones?" Nate asked.

"All of them. Not together, but in three separate groups."

"That's good news. There were the two couples and the three men." Now, I felt like we were making progress.

"Two groups of two men and the ladies with another man," Red said.

I looked at Nikki and then Nate. Did I hear they were mixed-up pairs and not what I thought they should have been?

"The two ladies went with this guy." Red tapped the picture of Eddie Capes. "Then this old dude," he pointed to Wilbur, "was with this guy."

"Wilbur Christy and Tom Holden were together?"

"I don't know their names, but then the other two went out later that same day." He handed me the cell phone.

"Todd Fisher and Felix Andrus. Do you remember when they rented the boat?"

"Boats. The ladies went out at the same time that nervous fella did, and it was maybe an hour after they got back. The remaining two went out after that. They all said they were going fishing, but they didn't take any bait, just poles and tackle." Red squinted into the sun. "Mighty fishy if ya ask me."

I nodded. "Has anyone else been asking questions about boat rentals?"

"Nope. I'm booked for the morning, but the afternoon is free. If they do, should I give you a jingle?"

"Please. Or Gage. And if they show up today, can you tell Gage which ones and when they left the dock and note their direction?"

He glanced at Nate. "I'm going out on the boom here and say something reeks, and it's not old bait?"

"Yes, don't ask questions. Lily can't tell you the answers anyway. Let's say the police department needs your help."

"I consider that my duty as a citizen."

"Thanks for your time, Red." I hadn't taken three steps when I turned back. "How did they pay you?"

"Funny you should ask. It was all small bills. I take nothing over a fifty if someone wants to pay cash." He gave an exaggerated wink. "More chance of funny money if you catch my drift."

I did. "Stick to your rules. Don't accept large bills. It's safer all around."

"I figure now you're wishing I had a credit card receipt. If they use one the next time they come back, I'll make a note of it for you, Lily."

"Thanks again, and remember, silence is golden." I ran a finger over my closed lips and Red gave me a thumbs up.

We walked to the parking lot without talking. I had many conflicting ideas that were giving me a headache and I couldn't think straight. All of them must be in on this together, and they've all been throwing the spotlight on the others as a distraction mode.

We stopped next to Nate's truck. "Thanks for tagging along with us today." I kissed his cheek.

He hugged me and then Nikki. "As usual, it

was interesting. Where do you take this information now, to Gage?"

"He was meeting with some people this morning, but he's coming to the bookstore for lunch. I'll fill him in then. You're coming over, right?"

"No. Let my mermaid know I need to pick up some supplies, so I'm running into Portland. Some lobster traps need repair, and I don't want to take the deckhands off the boat to pick them up. I should be back by mid-afternoon."

It was sweet that he was still calling my aunt his mermaid at seventy-plus. Having only been married a couple of years, they acted more like teenagers in love than seniors. Age didn't matter when it came to love.

"I'll let her know." We waved as he backed out of the parking spot. With a toot on the horn, he exited to the main road. "We've accomplished our two primary objectives, but I need to put everything we learned on the board. This makes little sense that the seven suspects knew each other well, and one of the six killed the seventh."

Nikki fell in step with me as we walked through the parking lot toward the town square. "Could it have been an accident, Todd Fisher's death? They threw the rock but didn't mean to kill him."

"I wouldn't think so. It would have needed a lot of force. We should ask EL how hard someone would have to be hit in the temple to cause more than an injury." Once we crossed the road, I withdrew my cell. "I'll text him."

EL, how much force does it take to kill someone with a rock in the temple? And come for lunch at the bookstore. Aunt Mimi brought food so we can talk about the case. See you soon!

I put the phone away.

Nikki watched me. "Aren't you going to wait for a response?"

"I'm just waiting for confirmation. If the angle of the rock impacted in the perfect spot, force is only part of the equation. It's like playing a game at the county fair. They're challenging to win unless you hit the target perfectly with the squirt gun."

"I never win at those games." She scuffed her feet, "But you're right, EL will confirm, not share, new information. That spot on the temple is small. I'm going to assume it's just the right spot, too."

We walked around the park on the brick path. I glanced at the bank as we went past. "I wonder if Gage talked with Chuck Yancy before the Secret Service showed up."

"I'm sure he was there the minute the bank opened," Nikki said. "That is an important part of the investigation. Speaking of, are we going to see William before heading back to the bookstore?"

I reversed direction. "Yes. We can walk past the other shops and see if anyone's talking about a rash of big bills being passed. You know, mid-morning is best for everyone to sweep the sidewalk."

"That's a diplomatic way of saying gossip time. The shops are ready for the day, but most visitors are lingering over breakfast."

I couldn't help but grin. "You know me too well, my friend."

She straightened her shoulders and pretended to adjust a hat. "Just call me Watson; I think it's much more appropriate. Don't you agree, Holmes?"

"Completely, Watson." With a new lightness in our step, we strolled toward the Sweet Spot.

Tucker wasn't outside the hardware store when we passed, but I noticed that the sidewalk was swept clean and even had a bit of water in puddles where he rinsed it down.

Next, Beatrice from Bee Bee's Boutique was sweeping her front step. "Good morning, girls. It's supposed to be another hot one today. I love summer, don't you?"

"It's one of my four favorite seasons," Nikki smiled.

"Aren't you quick with the quips this morning?" She grinned, "I may have to borrow that one of these days."

Nikki said, "Feel free."

We moved on to the Sweet Spot and opened the door. As usual, the aroma of yeast and cinnamon beckoned me to the display case. A tray of my favorite pecan cinnamon buns with a liberal slather of buttercream called to me. Since the tray was full, I knew they were fresh. I groaned and resigned myself to the fact I wasn't leaving here without one.

"Good morning, Jill. Is William around?"

"Hi, Lily, Nikki. He's in the back checking on a tray of muffins. Help yourself to a coffee and he'll be right out." Before she left, she plated two buns and placed a fork on each one. "Enjoy."

I glanced at Nikki. "Am I that transparent?"

"Jill's worked here for a while and knows your weakness." Nikki picked up the plates. "I'll get a table, and you get the coffee."

William came from behind and around the

counter, wiping his hands on a towel. "You wanted to see me, Lily?"

I pointed to the table. "Can you spare a few minutes? We need to talk."

His brow shot up. "This can't be good."

"It all depends." I placed the coffee cups on the table and dropped my voice. "This needs to be kept confidential for now."

Chapter 14
Lily

After savoring the first bite of pecan bun, I wiped my mouth with a napkin. I placed my hand on William's arm. "Has anyone tried to pay with a one-hundred-dollar bill in the last two weeks?"

"Sure. It's pretty normal for out-of-towners to use big bills. And I've accepted one recently. Why?"

"William, this is important. Do you know who you accepted the bill from, and if I showed you a picture, do you think you'd recognize him or her?"

"Lily, breathe. I took the bill from Chuck Yancy just this morning."

"Can I have it? You can charge the amount on my debit card."

With a wave of his hand, he smiled. "I'm not worried about the money, and if you feel you need to take the bill with you, then it's not a problem. But is this your way of suggesting I don't take anymore?"

"For the time being, yes."

He got up, went to the cash register, pulled the bill out, and returned to the table. "Here you go. I'll let Jill know we're not accepting large bills for a bit." He patted my hand. "Feel better?"

I exhaled. "Yes."

"Can you tell me what's going on?" He leaned closer. "I'm guessing it has to do with funny money?"

I kept my face expressionless, which would tell him more than words.

"Got it."

I withdrew my cell. "Can you tell me if

these people look familiar?" He had confirmed the three men, Todd, and Susan, had been in, but what about Simone and Tom?

William scrolled through the images. "They've all been in within the last few days. Two couples and the three men, but never as one group." He handed me my phone.

I felt better that he looked again. "Thanks for double checking."

"Does this have to do with the man who died? You know, at the station?"

"It does. He was in town with his wife. Or so we think."

Nikki said, "Lily will agree with me. Every time we think we're getting closer to who's who, the players shift in the family tree."

That was an excellent way to say it. "Right now, I'm going to concentrate on our snack and worry about the case later." I lifted my mug and took a sip of the comforting brew.

William pushed back the chair and stood. "I have muffins calling my name in the kitchen, but if you need something else, please let me know."

"Thanks, William." I gave him a frosting filled smile. "Excellent buns today, too."

"You say that every day." He tapped the top of the table and slipped away.

"Nikki, what do you think about all of this? Should we wait for people to come back and rent boats again?"

Her eyes widened. "Like a stakeout?"

"No, we'll leave that boring stuff to Jonesy and Jessie Sullivan."

"It could be exciting." She nodded out the window. "Don't look now, but we're about to have interesting company."

I moved my chair, so I had a clear view of the entrance. Tom and Simone pulled open the door and came inside.

At first, they looked only at the counter, but then Simone saw us and touched Tom's arm. "I'm going to say hello to the ladies."

"I'll get you an iced coffee."

"Thanks. Milk, two sugars." She crossed the room. "Hello, ladies, enjoying some time away from the grind?"

"We are, and you're out for a?" I let the question dangle.

"I agreed to a boat ride with Tom, so we're getting drinks and snacks before we head down to the boat rental. He promises we'll only be gone a few hours."

I noted her crisp jean shorts, a long-sleeve linen blouse, a wide-brimmed hat, deck shoes, and oversized sunglasses. Her outfit suggested she wasn't going fishing. Now, that was interesting.

Tom wandered in our direction and slid his arm around her waist. "Good morning, ladies. I didn't expect to see you until this afternoon. Simone plans on dropping some greenbacks at your bookstore."

"I hear you're going fishing." I caught a flash of surprise when he glanced at Simone.

"My beautiful wife has agreed to indulge me for a few hours." He hugged her close to his body, her arms wrapped around him. Her lips dipped into a frown before she smiled again. She reminded me of a kid who gets hugged by a great aunt he's never met.

"You never know what you might catch this time of year."

"We're hoping to get lucky and pull out a big one." He grinned. "Do you ladies fish much?"

"When we have the time. In fact, we were fishing on Sunday and pulled up an interesting catch."

Nikki's brows arched as I tried to bait the hook for the happy couple, but Tom seemed distracted as he glanced at the door and clock above it. "We should leave these ladies to enjoy their coffee break so we can get to the boat in time for our reservation. The sooner we go, the sooner we'll get back."

"You're right, dear. I'll be by the bookstore to shop. After all, Tom will owe me big for agreeing to go on this expedition."

"Hon, after thinking you'd almost lost me,

you said spending time together was your most important goal."

"And it is, but maybe someday you'll develop a better idea of what's fun for us both." She laughed, but there was an edge to it that was borderline nasty.

Fishing was the last thing on her list. "Enjoy the trip. The water's nice and smooth today, but don't forget to wear a life jacket. There are rogue waves, you know."

Simone glanced at Tom. "Is that bad? It sounds bad. What do we do if we get hit by a rogue wave?"

"Dear, please relax. I reserved a sturdy boat, and I'm sure it can withstand any waves. Hopefully, we can go out while it's still calm. If not, we'll have to wait. Then we'll fish for a couple of hours and come in. Besides, rogue waves are more apt to happen in winter than summer and hardly ever reach the shore."

The annoyed look he flashed me was comical, but at least he knew his ocean facts.

"Simone, I was teasing, and I'm sorry if I frightened you."

She stepped toward the counter. "Not funny." She shimmied her shoulders and exhaled a deep breath. "Tom, let's go before I change my mind." She picked up the white bakery bag and the to-go drink tray from the counter.

I wondered if they'd still stop in the bookstore later today. I guessed I'd have to wait and see. "Good luck."

She said, "We won't need luck. We have a fish tracker thing-ama-bob."

Tom ushered her out the door and let it close with a thud after them. They hurried around the corner in the direction of the marina.

"Now, that is very interesting, don't you think?"

Nikki sipped her coffee. "What did I miss? The GPS tracker?"

"No, she had to tell him how she took her iced coffee. Don't most spouses know how their significant other takes coffee after the first few months of dating?"

"I would think so." Nikki wiped her mouth with a paper napkin. "Something bugs me about those two."

"Would you care to share what?"

"One minute, they act like the perfect married couple, and the other is as if they don't know each other. Maybe they're newlyweds and had a short courtship."

I gave her a playful swat on the hand. "Courtship? Who uses that word today?"

She sniffed and lifted her chin. "I do, and I like it. It's sweet and reminds me of when Steve and I started dating before we fell in love."

"Don't get your wand in a flicker. I was poking at you because I adore you, and it's a word I would have used, too. There are two old-fashioned ladies at this table."

Her face relaxed into a smile. "But you get what I mean about Tom and Simone. There's something' off about them."

"I agree, and when we get back to the store,

we're going to do research to see what more we can find out about the happy couple, along with Todd and Susan Fisher. Like, why would the ladies have gone out with Eddie Capes on the boat?"

"Could Red have been mistaken about who went with who when he looked at the pictures?" Nikki finished her coffee and stuffed the wadded up napkin in the mug.

"I know the town doesn't have cameras everywhere like a city does, but maybe someone at the marina has a security camera that would have picked up who was going with who and when."

Nikki chuckled. "That was quite a tangle of words. Is it sad that I knew exactly what you meant?"

"Not at all. We're in sync with each other, and that's a wonderful thing." I stood and picked up our dishes. "Am I interrupting your baking today?"

"No. I got everything done before I met you at the bookstore. Sometimes being a witch is much more advantageous to small business owners like us."

I waved goodbye to William, who peeked out behind the swinging kitchen door. "See you tomorrow."

Outside, I said, "I don't use magic much at the bookstore. I find it soothing to put books on the shelves and move sections around."

She grinned. "Like doing housework?"

We both knew that when I first discovered I was a witch and could do household stuff using magic, I resisted, saying I wanted to continue doing everything the way I always had. Over time, I did more and more by magic, except for cooking. Apparently, I needed the kitchen witch gene, which I didn't have, to make a decent meal. Baked goods were another story. I had some edible recipes after I did the cranberry bake-off last November.

"Oh, I'm not a fool, but I am a quick study. I love that with a spell or flick of my wrist, I can get the house tidy in no time at all."

"And cooking?"

"Take out or Gage, for which Milo is eternally grateful. Sometimes I need to let go and realize that will never be in my cauldron of skills."

Nikki looped her arm through mine and laughed. "You've embraced all that there is to being a witch. I'm proud of you."

"Well, thank you." I pretended to wipe a tear from my eye.

"Brat. You don't need to fake being emotional." She tugged my arm.

We laughed all the way back to the store, and we were still chuckling when we walked in. Milo looked up from the window seat. "What's so funny?"

"Just having fun with my bestie."

Aunt Mimi was behind the counter. "Did you learn anything that will help solve the case?"

"Learned yes, solve no." I glanced around the store.

"We're alone," she said.

"I'm not sure if Nikki feels the same, but

the story becomes increasingly confusing as we uncover more. It seems our two couples know each other."

She looked between me and Nik. "What?"

I nodded. "Yes, and they know the men who were watching us as we investigated Todd Fisher's attack. They knew him. Why wouldn't they come to his aid?"

"Everyone knows everyone, and they knew the attacker and wanted to avoid the incident?"

I tapped my finger on the countertop. "Exactly. They knew who it was, and they're all connected. My money says they're involved up to their eyeballs and with the satchel, too."

Aunt Mimi said, "What time do you think everyone will be here? I don't want to be in the way."

I drew her into a hug. "You're never in the way, and I'm not sure. Since we just had coffee and a bun, hopefully, it will be a while. We're going to do some research in the back. Would you cover the shop?"

"I'm here as long as you need me." She

strolled to where Phoenix and Milo lounged in the window, watching the world go by.

At times, I envied Milo hanging out and eating fishy treats regularly. Having me as his witch might be challenging, but Milo was well loved. Taking my laptop from under the counter, I looked at Nikki. "Ready to take a deep dive into the lives of our couples?"

She rubbed her hands together. "Can't wait. Who are we going to check on first?"

That was an easy answer. "Simone and Tom. Like you said at the bakery, there's something off and it appears like a riptide. The surface looks safe, but underneath is another story."

An hour later, we were far from finding dirt on either couple. Tom Holden appeared to be a businessman, of what I couldn't tell. The social media site used for professional connections stated he was a consultant what was a dead end. Simone Holden was married to Tom, and other than serving on a few charity boards, it seemed she didn't work outside of the home.

This is interesting, I said, "Susan Fisher works in a bank. That seems to be an interesting coincidence. "Do you think it's possible someone who worked in a bank could launder fake bills for the real thing without getting caught?"

She said, "I don't know how a bank works, but it's possible if someone had regularly come to her window. Any luck on Todd Fisher and his background?"

"He drives an Uber in the metro area of Boston. At least that checks out. This search seems to confirm the Holdens don't have a permanent address. They move every year."

"He's a business consultant, maybe that's why. He has a new contract every year."

I tapped my chin. "That's a good point. The two tie it together. I wonder what Gage has discovered in his meeting with the federal agents."

"Probably more than he can tell us."

I heard the store door open, and Mimi said,

"Gage. It's good to see you. Lily's in the back. Oh, and I've prepared lunch for everyone."

"Thanks, Mimi." Gage entered the office combo storage room. Nikki pushed out a chair for him. He dropped into it and placed his head in his hands.

"How was the meeting with the feds?"

He looked at me. "You don't want to know."

Chapter 15
Gage

There was only so much I could tell Lily about the meeting. The most crucial details I had I couldn't share since the agents had sworn me to silence and secrecy. I was in the same boat with EL, Peabody, and Mac. How could I investigate and solve a murder without talking with my team?

Lily waited a few seconds, but I didn't say anything more. "We've had an interesting morning. At the moment, we're tracking down our two couples. Both live in Boston, but the Holdens move every year. We think it's because of his job as a business consultant. Todd Fisher drove an Uber."

I kept my face neutral, without a twitch or flinch, which would cause Lily to ask more questions I couldn't answer. "What did you discover at the marina?"

Mimi came into the room before Lily could answer. "I have lunch laid out, and I've hung up the closed sign so you can talk undisturbed."

"Thank you, Mimi." At least Lily could share the boat rental information, and I wouldn't need to worry about anyone inter-rupting us.

She picked up her handbag and said, "I'm meeting Nate at the Copper Kettle, but I'll be back later to cover the store."

"Mimi, you don't need to leave. Besides, Nate had to drive to Portland."

She looked from me to the ladies. "I do. There are undercurrents I don't want to pre-tend I don't know about if asked later." She placed her hand on my arm. Instantly, a calm came over me. "Gage, you need Lily's help more than ever."

How did she know my hands were tied, and I wasn't sure which direction to move in? "Enjoy your lunch." It was a feeble comment, but all I could think of.

She waved with a flutter of her fingertips. "Toodles."

Lily and Nikki stood, taking the laptop as they entered the main room. Mimi had set up a small banquet table with sandwiches, cut-up fruit and vegetables, and a plate of cookies. She had also placed carafes of what I assumed was hot coffee and pitchers of iced tea and water on the table.

Mimi sailed out the door, as Mac, EL, and Sharon entered.

Mac gave a low, appreciative whistle. "This is quite a spread." He picked up a paper plate and filled it with everything that would fit. "Mimi's a treasure." He jabbed my arm. "You're lucky to be marrying into that family."

He didn't know half of how lucky I was. I

smiled at Lily, who gave me a saucy wink. "Dig in, everyone, and then we can hear what Lily and Nikki discovered this morning. I, for one, can't wait."

Her brows knitted together, and I realized I had just gone over the top with my compliment. "Well, since we were tied up this morning with our guests, you two were the only ones working the actual case." I wasn't sure if she would buy that statement, but it was the best I could come up with.

Sharon said, "Lily, it was nice of Mimi to make everyone lunch. She didn't need to go to so much trouble."

"My aunt loves feeding people and whipped this up in no time." Lily picked up plates and passed them to EL and Nikki before she handed one to me. "Save room for a cookie, the sugar cookies are perfection."

EL stacked two on the edge of his plate. "You don't need to tell me twice." He sat next to Sharon. I moved a small side table in front of them to share.

Once we were all settled with our meal, Lily said, "Dang, I need to get my board."

Before she could get up, I was already moving toward the back room. "I've got it." I came back and got it set up. When I looked, she was staring at me.

"You'd better tell me what's got your cauldron bubbling before you burst."

Sharon snickered, "I like that: cauldron bubbling, like at the haunted house."

I glanced her way. "We should help at the Halloween event again this year."

Lily's voice was laced with annoyance as she said, "Gage Erikson. What's going on?"

I dropped my head. So much for keeping a secret that I was withholding information. "Lily, it's not what you think."

She cocked a brow. "Maybe I should be the judge of that."

EL leaned into Sharon. "She must be tough to surprise for her birthday."

Sharon shushed him. "Leave them be."

I cleared my throat. "Here's the thing, and

this doesn't just go for me but for the team, too."
I nodded to EL, Sharon, and Mac. "We're not allowed to discuss anything about the satchel or the people involved. We still have jurisdiction over the death of Todd Fisher if it doesn't interfere."

"Interfere with what? The feds' investigation?"

I knew that tone in Lily's voice; all I had done was get her mind spinning. "We can't do anything with the forged money right now," I said.

She popped a slice of cucumber in her mouth, and I saw a glint come into her eye. "It's a good thing I'm not an official police officer. No one can tell me what I can or can't do."

It felt like I had baited a hook, and she took it. "Lily, this is a much bigger issue than we've seen before."

With a dismissive wave, she took a bite of her sandwich and crossed to the board. She picked up a marker. "Since you can't investigate how the clues come together, Nikki and I will tie this up in a nice neat bow for you. When you make the arrest, I'm assuming the feds will be happy and take the credit. For now, I'll give you a rundown on what we've uncovered."

She drew arrows connecting Simone, Susan, and Eddie. Changing the color of the marker she did the same with Tom and Wilbur, and Felix and Todd. "These three groups each rented a boat from Red at different times to go fishing. They paid for the rental in small bills. The question is, for people who claim they don't know each other, why would they take a boat ride together? Oh, and no bait."

Mac said, "They lied."

She jabbed the marker in his direction. "Precisely. Remember when Susan, pretending to be Simone, first identified Todd as Tom? They had to have known each other, or she wouldn't have pulled that name out randomly. Why didn't she say who he really was? She wanted to misdirect the police. Also, she's not staying at the B & B so she wouldn't have stumbled across them in the dining room over coffee. Finally, Tom and Todd were dressed alike."

Sharon nodded. "This is true. But why would the married couples not be together, and how are Eddie, Wilbur, and Felix connected to these couples?"

"It's obvious they planned to be here together. But why?"

Nikki shot her hand in the air. "It's about the object that can't be named."

Lily circled the word satchel on her board. "Yes! Five points to the lady eating watermelon." She wrote a number one on the board. Next to it, she wrote, *Not strangers.*

"The next curious thing. No one approached Donnie White, but while talking with him at his slip, Keith Hanson mentioned he chatted with a group of people at the market looking for a boat rental. They said they wanted to take the boat out themselves, and he gave them Red's information. And for the record, he thought they were up to no good."

Mac said, "For Keith to say something like that, it must have been obvious."

I nodded. "This is great information. Did you learn anything else?"

She grinned. "Nikki, would you care to share about our last stop on the clue tour?"

"I'd be happy to." She stood and pointed to the shoulder bag on the counter. "Lily, would you care to get the money? I believe you have a special UV light in your register."

What were they up to?

She tossed Nikki the marker. "You have the floor, my dear Watson."

Nikki smiled. "After we left the marina, we wanted to check in with William to see if anyone had tried to pay with a large bill, particularly a one-hundred-dollar bill. Yesterday, we asked about the visitors in town, but not the cash. He took one this morning, which he didn't find odd."

I sat up straighter in the chair. "Is it a fake, and who did he get it from?"

"That's what we're about to find out." Nikki gestured to Lily. "What's the verdict?"

Flashing the light over the bill, she grinned, "Phony." She waved it before handing me the bill and the UV light.

I passed the light over it and handed it to EL. He showed it to Sharon, who passed it on to Mac.

"Lily, who paid William with this bill?"

She crossed her arms over her chest and smirked. "None other than the new VP at the bank, Chuck Yancy."

"You're kidding. What was he doing with it?"

She flashed me a triumphant look. "That's the question I intend to ask him since you can't."

I shook my head. "No. You're not going anywhere near him. It's information we need to turn over to Agents Flores and Peters."

Her eyes widened. "Peters, like Dax?"

Well, that cat was out of the bag. "His cousin,

Althea, and to answer your next question before you ask, they are almost identical." I hoped she caught my drift that Althea was a witch.

Nodding, she said, "That is an interesting twist." Tapping her finger to her lips, she strolled to the windows. "I wonder."

"Lily, what are you thinking?"

She sat down next to Milo, and he began to purr loudly. Which meant he was giving his witch an opinion about the situation.

She asked, "Gage, are the agents remaining in town?"

"Yes, what's running through your complex brain?"

Kissing Milo on the head, she walked back to the board. Taking another long look at it, she said, "We should invite the agents to have dinner with us tomorrow. I won't have enough time to prepare the invite for tonight." She gave a warm smile to Mac, EL, and Sharon. "Of course, you'll come, too." She snapped her fingers. "Nikki and I will plan the entire thing. Let's say five o'clock."

"Lily, is this a friendly dinner or working?" Mac said, "Should I bring Margaret?"

"Absolutely friend zone. I'll even see if Dax is free."

"Lily."

Due to the rumble in my voice, she glanced at me. "Trust me, I won't get you into any trouble. It would be rude not to invite them for a decent meal."

The innocent look didn't fool me, but I wouldn't try to have this conversation with my team in the room. If she understood Althea was a witch, would she lean into that connection to convince Althea that she and Nikki were assets?

"Is the other agent, Flores, is she related to anyone we know?"

"Not that I'm aware of." I took a large bite of my sandwich and did my best not to let her penetrating gaze unnerve me.

Sharon said, "Since we can't help you with what you're doing, effectively, we're hands-off until something new comes to light.

Have you uncovered anything that might help us?"

Lily pulled a chair up next to EL. "What have you discovered from the autopsy? Do you think it was deliberate or just a simple accident?"

"The force of the blow and direction of impact led me to conclude it wasn't accidental. Based on the sand and lichen samples I've taken, the rock we found at the scene is from the jetty. Of course, this is just preliminary results, but I'm confident in my findings."

"Can you get fingerprints from a rock?"

EL shifted, obviously uncomfortable, in his seat and looked at me. "You can, but in this instance, the prints were hard to read."

"Why?" Lily wasn't about to let up on this line of questions until she had the answer she was looking for.

"A few reasons are typical. If the person had used a chemical like antibacterial lotion, it could make it difficult, or in a cold climate, skin is dry from the weather, so oils aren't as present, or the person is older."

"What does an older hand have to do with prints?" Nikki asked.

EL set his plate down. "As skin ages, the ridges become worn, and getting a reliable print is harder."

Lily went back to the board. "And our rock. Good prints or not?"

I nodded at him when he looked in my direction. We discovered this information before the agents imposed the gag order.

"I can't get decent prints off the rock. It'll get sent out to the federal lab at Quantico."

"EL, an educated guess? The prints were wiped, possibly by someone using a substance or an older person."

He gave Lily an assessing gaze. "Are you asking me for an opinion or fact?"

"Opinion."

Sharon said, "EL deals in facts, Lily—not speculation. I think your question is unfair."

Mac leaned forward. "But Lily has a valid point. EL has proven many times his instincts with evidence are unparalleled. I'd like to hear his opinion."

Peabody leveled her gaze at him. "You're encouraging her, Mac."

I wanted to stop the banter, but Lily was right. EL's opinion was appropriate in this case. "We should hear what EL has to say."

Sharon threw up her hands and crossed to the food table, picking up a sugar cookie and pouring herself a coffee. I surmised this was her way of staying out of Lily's line of questions. Sharon didn't have more information than what had already been shared.

Leaning forward, with his hands clasped between his knees, EL said, "It is my opinion that it was a chemical or someone who is older."

Lily clapped her hands together. "Or both." She wrote next to Wilbur's name, *old and uses hand sanitizer.*

I saw where she was going with her train of

thought. "Team, we need to bring in Wilbur Christy for another round of questioning, one of which was when he was last at the jetty."

Lily said, "Now we're following the right clues."

Chapter 16
Lily

Gage shook his head. "Lily, I appreciate all you've done, but you can't be at the station while we question Wilbur Christy."

I stamped my foot on the ground. "Darn it. Why not? If it weren't for this conversation, you wouldn't be moving in his direction."

"True, but with our special guests in town, I received a directive I can't ignore."

I looked at Nikki, and she winked. There was a way around this newly imposed exile. "That's fine, but just remember, if there is something you can tell me, I expect all the pertinent details."

Gage's cell phone rang. He moved closer to the back room. "Erikson."

I kept one eye on him as I pretended to study the board. He was nodding and pacing, which was never a good combination. He ran a hand over his short hair and said, "We'll meet you there in fifteen minutes."

He stashed the phone back in his pocket. "Lunch is over. We're needed at the station."

"Why?" I attempted to keep the question casual since there was no way I could tag along.

He kissed me on the lips. "Sorry, Sweetheart. It has to remain confidential."

"All right, at least let me know when you'll bring in Wilbur Christy for questioning."

He nodded. "Be careful today. These people we're dealing with aren't the average person who just accidentally killed someone in a fit of rage."

I held up my hand in the scout's salute. "Promise."

Sharon and Mac were on their feet and close on Gage's heels as he strode out the front door.

"Thanks for lunch," Sharon called over her shoulder as she waved to EL, who wandered over to the food table, picked up two additional cookies, and poured himself a coffee before he sat down, crossed his legs, and settled in.

I stole a glance at Nikki, and she lifted her shoulder in a shrug. He never hung out with us. I always got the impression he was slightly uncomfortable around us.

Breaking a cookie in half, he dunked it in the coffee and closed his eyes as he savored the bite. "Mimi is very talented in the kitchen."

"She's a wonderful cook." I decided that since he wasn't in a hurry to leave, maybe we could pick his brain about the money, victim, or rock. Heck, anything at this point would help narrow our focus.

Nikki and I settled into the wingback chairs. I asked, "You don't need to rush off?"

He shook his head. "Not right now. There

are so many questions rolling around in my head. Enjoying a cuppa coffee and a cookie will clear my thoughts."

"I agree. There's nothing like something sweet with a good cup of hot bean water," Nikki said.

"That's right. You're something of an expert in the kitchen yourself." He seemed casual in this vein of conversation, but there was something in his undertone that put my guard up. "How do you get so much accomplished every day? You must have an amazing system."

The hair on the back of my neck stood at attention. "Nikki's the best at organizing. In fact, she helps me from time to time in the bookstore."

He nodded. "It's good to have friends so talented at so many things."

I wanted to ask him point blank what he was getting at, but I felt he suspected something that, as a non-magical, we couldn't confirm or deny.

"Would it be possible to order a cake?

Sharon has a birthday next month, and I thought it would be nice to surprise her with one of your delicious confections."

With a smile, Nikki crossed her legs and gave EL her undivided attention. "I'd be happy to bake a birthday cake. Do you have any idea about the flavor of the cake and frosting? What about a filling? How many people should it serve?"

"Ten to twelve people. I'm hoping the group will get together for dinner at my place. She adores chocolate, and as far as I know, she doesn't have any food allergies. I'll leave the rest in your capable hands."

"Not to worry, her taste buds will weep with joy. When will you have the party?"

"The thirtieth."

"I'll put that on my calendar." Nikki pulled out her phone and tapped a few keys.

"Now I just have one question," a glint shone in his eyes, "Will you bake it the human way or the witch way?"

I did a double take. Had he just come out and asked Nikki if she was a witch?

"Don't look so surprised; your secret is safe with me." With a snap of his fingers, the plate of cookies floated to his lap.

"How did you do that?" I eked out.

"Come on, Lily, I know you're a witch, too." He held out the plate. "Cookie?"

Nikki stood up. "We don't know what you're talking about, but you're scaring the bah-zeeies out of us." She slid next to me and clutched my hand.

The best way to play this was denial until we knew for sure which side of the broom he sat. "EL, I'm not sure what you think you know, and I'm also not sure how you got that plate of cookies in your lap. It might be time for you to return to your lab." I squeezed Nikki's hand even tighter. The last time I felt this nervous around someone who did magic was when the magicians had rolled through town, and it was for a valid reason.

He set aside his coffee mug and placed the

cookie plate next to it. Rising to his feet, he said, "If you say so. I feel the surge when you've performed spells. It's your signature that gave you away. Remember this—you don't need to be afraid of me or anyone else in this town. You're Lily Michaels. And Nikki Twing, as her best friend, you will continue to stand at her side. All I ask is to be included in what you do." He picked up another cookie. "One for the road."

After he was outside and the door was firmly closed, I sagged into a chair. "What do you make of all of that? And do I surge?"

"We need to ask Mimi if EL Dawson is registered as a witch and part of our coven but never attends meetings."

"Oh, good. That was my next question. If you've ever seen him at one."

She shook her head. "No. But I'm more concerned with why he stepped from the shadows now? It makes no sense."

"And this surge?"

Nikki gave me a sheepish grin. "Yeah, your signature is like a neon sign. It's kinda cool. But not to worry. Those who know you're learning have accepted it as a normal occurrence. In fact, it gives my magic a boost."

I rubbed my eyes. When was my magic going to be ordinary? There was no time to dwell on what energy my spells gave off. There was a murder to solve, and fast.

"We have bigger issues than EL's witch status. We must figure out who killed Todd Fisher and why. Gage's hands are tied, but ours aren't."

The front door burst open, and Aunt Mimi sauntered in. "I'm back! I've been across the street in the town square waiting until the last police person left. And was that EL I saw leaving by himself?'

"It was. Do you know him, Aunt Mimi?"

"Not well, but recently, it's come to my attention that EL wants to join our coven."

"So, he's a witch?" Nikki asked.

"Apparently, but from what the rumor mill is dispersing, he's been non-practicing for years. Something about wanting to live in the non-magical world as one of them." She shuddered. "I can't imagine giving up a large part of who you are. It's like shutting down one of your senses." She waved her hand through the air. "Never mind my ramblings. How was the meeting, and did you have enough food?" She scanned the buffet table. "There aren't many leftovers, and I see the cookies were a hit."

"Everyone was hungry and appreciated the spread." I glanced at Nikki before looking at Mimi again. "About EL?"

"Don't worry about him, but did you tell him you're both witches?"

"No. We denied it."

Nikki said, "We didn't know if it was safe or if he was baiting us even when he moved the plate of cookies by magic. I've never met someone who fishes for information like he did."

Nodding in agreement, I said, "Me, too. It reminded me of the magicians when they strolled into my bookstore."

"I'll check his background and let you

know. Being prudent is never a bad thing. Speaking of bad guys, are you any closer to solving the case of who killed that man?"

I exhaled with a heavy sigh. "No, and Gage can't discuss the case with us anymore. Heck, they're not supposed to talk to anyone except the agents in town. But there is a bright spot; I'm going to host a dinner party tomorrow night for the agents and our friends. It might help uncover some details Gage couldn't tell me."

"That is an excellent idea." With a flick of her wrist, the food was stacked in glass containers.

"The kicker: one of the agents is Dax's cousin, Althea."

Aunt Mimi's brow quirked. "Really? Now that is interesting. I wonder if he filled her in on the goings on in town."

"I'm sure. I'm going to see if he can join us."

She clapped her hands together. "It sounds like a fun evening, even if you're trying to get someone to spill beans." Pointing to the door, she waved. "Now, the two of you need to hit the streets and follow clues or whatever it is you like to do. Maybe work on wedding plans or sit on the beach. I've got the store for the afternoon."

I kissed her cheek. "Aunt Mimi, how did I get so lucky to be born into this family?"

"Luck had nothing to do with it, my dear. You were destined to be here." She flicked her finger in the door's direction, and it opened. "Run along."

Grinning, I looked at Nikki. "Some beach time sounds like fun, and we can mull over a few ideas, too."

"The beach sounds perfect. Pack your wedding planner, and we'll go over the details."

Laughing, I asked, "Nikki, are you trying to divert my train of thought?"

She tipped her head. "Maybe. It's better than you beating yourself up for not knowing what the police know."

"I'm thinking we could beach it near the marina, so if someone happened to rent a boat, we could get some photos to add to my board." I called, "Milo, do you want to come, or will you meet me at home?"

Giving a grumbled response from somewhere in the store, "I'm sleeping, and sand gets everywhere. No thank you."

That answered that question. "See you at home later."

No response.

"Nikki, let's go be beach bums."

Sitting under an umbrella in our beach chairs, Nikki and I sported wide-brimmed hats, large dark sunglasses, and plenty of sunscreen. It might be Maine, but I didn't want to be as red as a lobster by the end of the afternoon.

While Nikki was setting up our spot, I popped over to see Red to inquire if anyone, mainly our suspects, had rented a boat. He was waiting for Tom and Simone, but as of a half hour ago, they hadn't shown up. The day was still young, with plenty of time for them to 'go fishing.'

"I forgot to ask Aunt Mimi about my magic causing a surge."

Nikki brushed sand from her hands. "It'll keep for today. It's nothing to worry about; if it were, I'd tell you."

I considered her response and pushed it aside. There was one thing I could count on concerning magic and Nikki—she always had my back. "Consider the topic tabled for now."

"What do you think the chances are we'll discover someone carrying fishing poles and buckets of bait?"

With a snort, I slid my sunglasses down my nose. "When pigs fly?"

I had a book in my lap, but my eyes never left the docks. I'd see whoever was in search of a rental boat the minute they slunk over the wood planks.

The minutes ticked by, and all was quiet. Nikki shifted in her chair. "Since we don't have any suspects on the move, let's talk wedding."

Smiling, I put my glasses aside. "Can you believe we'll both be married women in a few weeks?" I didn't attempt to disguise the wonder in my voice. "I always thought Gage would end up marrying someone else, a girl I had to hate because she dared to say how she felt. Now, I'm that girl and marrying the man of my dreams." I placed my hand over my heart and sighed.

Quietly, she said, "Put your sunglasses on. We have company."

I pushed them up the bridge of my nose and casually looked around. There was Tom and Simone, strolling down the dock hand in hand.

"On their six, we have a quartet watching them."

I swiveled my gaze to survey the parking area. Eddie and Susan were on one bench, and Wilbur and Felix were on another. "All the pawns are in place on the board."

When I spoke with Red, I asked if I could leave a microphone under a seat. I promised to use it only if the suspects rented the boat. As my book had suggested, I added a dash of magic to enhance the spell.

He'd eagerly agreed. He didn't want his reputation tarnished by the group of unsavory characters.

Picking up my cell, I pretended to send a text while finalizing the eavesdropping spell. *Magnify a witch's ears to hear voices of those up to no good. Listening is best when it comes close to an arrest. For this I wish, so it shall be.*

"We plan to be out for a couple of hours." Bingo, it was Tom's voice, and he was talking to Red. "Here's your money. I hope cash is okay. You know, people can clone credit cards these days. It's never good to take too many chances."

Since Red was a good guy, I couldn't hear his voice.

"I remember how to run the boat. Thanks again." Then Tom said, "Simone, cast off the stern and bow lines, and we can get this tug underway."

"Why do I always have to do the grunt work?"

His laugh was anything but friendly. "I'm the brains of our merry band, and the rest of you do the work. It's how it's been and how it will continue to be."

I heard what I believe were the bowlines thump on the deck and another thump on the stern.

"Simy, push off. I don't want to be out too long. I hate the sun."

"You and every other vampire."

Simone had a sharp tongue, unlike the demur woman we had initially met. I glanced at Nikki to see if she was hearing all of this. She had taken off her sunglasses and was sitting on the side of the chair, her feet in the sand, leaning close to me.

I gave her a wink. "This is about to get interesting."

Chapter 17
Lily

The boat eased away from the dock. I wished I was on it instead of just my listening spell in action. Even with the added dose of magic, I wasn't sure if the spell had a range of effectiveness. Surely, Nikki would have mentioned it if that was the case. She gave me a thumbs up, and I took that to mean we would get the scoop of the day.

Tom and Simone discussed their lunch at the Copper Kettle and criticized the lobster bisque. They had the nerve to say they thought the meat was imitation. I held back a laugh. A cauldron calling the kettle black.

"Can you believe the prices around this town?" Simone said. "From the pastries that lady Nikki makes to a simple cup of tea. It's all good, but really? You'd think we were in the city."

Was she talking about my mom's special blends? I wanted to say that everything here is freshly produced, either caught, grown, or handcrafted. But I would be shouting into the wind. The boat was puttering out of the harbor.

"Small towns can be expensive. We've seen it before. I've enjoyed our meals, and considering why we're here, this would have been a nice place to vacation if we weren't working."

"You would." She stopped talking and sat in the co-captain's seat as he maneuvered out of the no-wake zone.

I turned in my chair to keep my eyes on the boat. It was going to be a test of patience. I had never been a huge fishing fan unless I was on

Gage's boat with our friends, and it was a party. But I was out to hook a killer, so I'd sit here all afternoon if necessary.

The boat had grown smaller as it bobbed on the waves, and from where I sat, I wasn't sure how far out it was. Nikki handed me a pair of binoculars, and I lifted them, adjusting the view. Tom was fiddling with a dial on a black box, and he pointed to the right. Simone cast a line into the water and sat in the chair. It was like watching a small television screen in a large room. At least I could make out the essential movements. "This was a good idea."

"A bottomless beach bag always is." Nikki leaned forward. "What's happening?" I could hear the lilt of excitement in her voice.

"Tom is tuning a radio, I think, and Simone just dropped a line in the water."

She tapped my knee. "Think about what you just said, and don't think literally; go beyond what you see."

I lowered the binoculars. "He's trying to locate the bag using a GPS tracker."

She sat back and grinned. "Did Simone bait the hook?"

"Not that I could see." I looked their way again.

Tom's voice came in loud and clear. "Simone, recast the line to the left."

She stood, reeled the line in before casting it to the left, and once again sat down, propped up her feet, and tipped her face to the sun. This was hardly the pose of a fisherwoman who'd want to keep an eye on the line to see if anything tugged on it.

"How long do we have to be out here?"

Tom glanced up and looked at the water. "Seems like it'll take hours. We'll need to move around a few times, but with some luck, I hope we'll get a hit quick."

She leveled her gaze at him. "If we don't, can we call this adventure a loss and move on? There's another job waiting for us."

"I don't like leaving assignments open-ended." He tugged on the dangling line. "Slack. I thought it would drift and catch."

Dropping her feet to the boat deck, she set the pole aside. "Are you getting a signal?"

He shook his head. "Nothing." He took his ball cap off and ran a hand over his head. "Fifteen more minutes here before we move on."

He walked up the middle of the boat and stood on the bow with the black box. I couldn't see his face, but the set of his shoulders told me he was getting more frustrated. He kept tapping his fingers on the box. Since the bag wasn't in the water, this would be an uneventful adventure for them.

Simone grabbed the pole. "Hey, get over here now!"

Tom scrambled through the narrow aisle and rushed as fast as possible to her side.

"Got something?"

She had the pole in her hands and was reeling it in. "Help me."

He took the pole and cranked on the reel, moving the rod forward as if he were playing with the fish to tire it. "We didn't get a hit on the bag. The signal must have died."

"Nik, they think they got something."

She said, "Don't look now, but the peeps in the peanut gallery are on their feet with binoculars, too. It seems this is the most exciting thing to happen this afternoon."

"You watch them, and I'll stay focused on Tom and Simone."

"You got it, Sherlock."

I grinned but didn't look away from Tom and the fishing pole.

He said, "It's getting closer."

I could hear the excitement ramp up in his voice. A fluttering filled my stomach, and my pulse quickened. What could they be bringing up from the bottom?

"It's heavy."

"The bag's waterlogged. Of course, it's heavy." Simone leaned over the edge. She held a net in her hand.

"Almost here." He was cranking on the reel for all it was worth. "Get ready." He stumbled back, and Simone's arm disappeared over the side of the boat.

He dropped the pole and rushed to her side, steadying the handle of the net. With a grunt, the net and a bright blue bag landed on the deck.

"They pulled a bag from the water." I wasn't sure why I whispered. I couldn't take my eyes off Simone, Tom, and the bag that resembled a backpack.

Simone pulled it from the net. "Wait a minute, I thought it was brown? Were there two bags?"

"Not that I'm aware of, and I was told it was brown leather. This can't be it." He knelt next to the bag and tugged at the zipper.

I nudged Nikki. "He's opening the backpack."

She turned from watching the others, and I handed her the binoculars. "Look and tell me what you see." I had my cell phone out, ready to text Gage so he could hurry to the docks for the arrest.

"It looks like they pulled out a teddy bear, a plastic bag of something that might have been food; it looks green now. Wait, Simone is reaching around Tom."

"Just great. A dead end." Simone picked up the bag and heaved it into the water.

He sat back on his heels. "Why did you do that?"

"It's not what we're looking for, and any normal fishing expedition always throws back what they can't keep."

"Some kid's probably missing his teddy bear."

"Tom's leaned over the side, but the bag was out of reach." It was good that Nikki was filling me in. I put my phone away. This was not police officer worthy.

Handing me the binoculars, she said, "I'll keep my eye on the others."

Simone flopped into the seat. "Stop being a sentimental sap, and let's move the boat since this spot is a dud."

"Give me a few minutes to work on the box. Something's off."

She crossed her arms over her chest. "Have

you ever thought about the possibility that the bag could have drifted on the current and not be where it's supposed to be?"

"It's only been a few days. We haven't had any storms to whip up the current. Todd said this is the approximate location, so it must be somewhere here."

"Why you trusted him is beyond me." Adjusting her hat and sunglasses, Simone held her hand out and wriggled her fingers. "Let me see if I can get a signal."

He slapped the box in her palm, went to the captain's chair, kicked over the engine, and trolled up the coast. I adjusted the binoculars to maintain as clear a view as possible. "I wish they'd say something. How two people can be in the same boat and not have a conversation is beyond me?"

"Not every couple is like us, talking our partner's ears off."

I laughed and glanced at her. "True."

After a few minutes, the boat dropped anchor. But Tom continued to sit. "Simone, do you ever think we're in the wrong business?"

Dang, this listening spell was the bomb. It was like I was sitting on the boat with them. "Can you still see them?"

Nikki nodded. "Yes, and hear them, too. I hope you remember this spell. It could come in handy at another time."

"Do you think she wants to leave the forgery business?"

Lowering the other set of binoculars, Nikki's expression grew thoughtful. "When we first met the Holdens, I thought they were just a pleasant couple. But as we've continued to poke into the case, and after learning they've been in cahoots with the others all this time, either I'm jaded or a bad judge at first impressions."

I could picture my clue board in my mind. "I thought Todd Fisher was the leader of the forgery group. It made sense once we realized the men in the park and Susan all knew each other."

"And now?"

Her question had me wondering, "Why do you think Todd was killed?"

"He knew too much, or maybe he was the one who ditched the satchel with the brilliant idea they'd get it later." I pressed my finger to my lips. "Shh."

"Tom, this line of work has its difficulties. We both understood that when we became part of the business. But we're here now and have to see it through."

He nodded, and she pulled his head to her. "When it's over, can we change the path we're on?"

Tom looked at her. "I'm not sure we'll get that chance. Everything has gone wrong since we got involved. I don't know if we'll ever be able to walk away." He picked up the GPS box. "Let's just finish the job and get back to shore. You wanted to stop by that bookstore, and I have to meet with the group and fill them in."

Simone shaded her eyes and looked toward the shore. "Do you think they're sitting on benches waiting for us to come in?"

"You're kidding, right? I'd bet my last real dollar they'll be at the slip, wanting to know if we got the bag."

"What are you going to tell them?"

"The truth as we know it and then spin something back to Todd, like he must have used a faulty GPS tracker, and we might never find the satchel."

I slapped my thigh and wished I had recorded this. He proved my theory that he was working with the rest and knew the money was forged. This information wasn't enough to arrest him, but it was darn good.

I leaned back in the chair and tucked the binoculars in Nikki's bag, leaving the speaker on my phone connected by magic to the boat.

She did the same. "What's next?"

"We know there's nothing to find, and they're looking for the satchel. Tom and Simone were recruited for the operation but now have second thoughts. Unfortunately, they haven't revealed how or why Todd Fisher was killed. Why not? They're in the middle of nowhere, just the two of them. Don't you think now would be the perfect opportunity to discuss it?"

"Maybe they will." She nodded to the benches. "Those men and maybe Susan, too, know what happened to Todd Fisher."

"I wonder if they know what Tom and Simone found, or should I say, didn't find?"

Nikki jabbed her finger in their direction. "Yeah, it's easy to see they're fascinated by everything going on in that boat."

The sound of a cell phone ringing came through the speaker. Susan brought her hand to her ear.

Simone said, "Hello, Susan. We wanted to let you know we have discovered nothing out here. The signal to the package is non-existent. We're calling it a day."

I wished I knew how to have two spells running concurrently, but I could only sustain my magical focus on one at a time.

"We're all disappointed, but there's nothing more we can do today. We're headed in."

I could hear Simone, but I watched Susan react as she tumbled back to the bench.

"We are. You and the three stooges better evaporate. We can't have the locals seeing us together. It arouses too much suspicion."

She paused again and smacked a hand on her forehead. "If we had found the satchel, you would have seen us pull it from the water since you were gawking at us, and we'd be on our way to shore. If you think you and the stooges can do better, then, by all means, take the box and head out into the ocean. We're done wasting our time."

Susan's wild gestures with one arm made me imagine she was giving Simone a hard time because she wasn't doing better. Was Susan running this operation and not the Holdens? I was confused. So many things didn't add up.

"Let Red know you want to take the boat out. We're going to do a little poking around downtown to see if anyone has heard of the bag being discovered. We can meet later, say seven, at the Clam Shack? It's big enough that people shouldn't notice if our tables are close together."

Wilbur, Felix, and Eddie were standing now.

"We'll get there in plenty of time to secure tables close to each other."

Susan's hand fell to her side, and it was an easy assumption that the call was over. She pointed to the marina entrance to their right, and I refocused on the open line of communication with the boat.

"That didn't go well," Tom said. "Why meet them for dinner?"

"Don't you want to know which one smashed the side of Todd's head in? I do. If we have to get more involved with this operation because that bag is gone, I want to know who we're dealing with and who can lose control."

"We've come so far to be nowhere." He revved the boat engine and turned to the marina.

I glanced at Nikki. "We need to get to the

bookstore. If there's one thing Simone will do this afternoon, that's shop."

Nikki quickly gathered our belongings in her beach bag. I closed the umbrella, and she had already dealt with the beach chairs.

"Give me a minute. I want to send Gage a quick message. If we can discover who killed Todd Fisher, we'll know who's running the forging operation."

Chapter 18
Gage

My cell pinged with a text. I didn't glance up or break eye contact with Agent Nola Flores.

"Detective Erikson, do you need to get that?"

"It can wait. Please continue." Even though I knew that was Lily's unique tone, it had to wait. Nola was about to share everything she knew regarding the three men I had interviewed about Todd Fisher's death.

She gave me a curt nod and paced the area along the conference room table. "Felix Andrus, Eddie Capes, and Wilbur Christy are known associates of a well-known crime family. One couple," she stared at me to make sure I understood she was referring to the Secret Service's undercover agents, "were higher within the organization than those three but not as high as we'd like. There's a woman, Sophia, who's the niece to the head of the family. She's well respected and has the ear of her uncle. She's currently operating under an assumed name to conceal her identity. We're just not sure what name she's using or where she is."

"Why are they here in Pembroke Cove, of all places? We're a quiet little town only known for our lobster, just like every other coastal town in Maine."

Althea glanced at Nola. "We believe our agents deliberately steered the group here to get them to try to pass the bills. In a smaller town, it's easier for the bank to catch and trace them back to the origin."

I stood and whipped out my crime board. Tapping on Chuck Yancy's name, I said, "He's the only person we've been able to trace a forged bill to."

Althea raised a brow. "Gage, you know that he's a prime suspect. With his position at the bank, it would be easy for him to be dirty, and he's new in town."

I hung my head before looking them in the eye. "I want these people out of my town. If you need to arrest them all, go for it. If not, I'll instruct my officers to arrest them for littering or jaywalking or bug the heck out of them so they'll leave."

Nola placed her hands, palm side down, against the table and leaned closer. "And what of Todd Fisher? You're going to overlook the obvious fact—one of them killed him."

"There is no concrete evidence pointing to who did what. Our cameras caught him stumbling up the walkway, holding his head with one hand and dropping the rock with the other. He fell face-first onto the sidewalk. Dead. There was no car, no people, and worse, the only potential witnesses I have aren't talking other than to say his crazy wife did it." I thumped the tabletop with a fist. "I have no evidence tying her to the crime."

"Where was his wife before the crime?" Althea asked.

"Not here. Cameras can prove she wasn't near the park. The owner of the Copper Kettle stated she got a coffee and scone to go. Which doesn't put her close enough to the station to have been the attacker."

"Many people buy coffee and still have time to commit a crime." Nola pulled out a chair and sat down. "Gage, you don't want to arrest her, but you must. Ask the tough questions. If for no other reason than for her protection."

I clicked the projector screen remote and tapped a few keys on my laptop. "Did you read in the autopsy that the attacker had to be roughly five ten or taller? Both women are too short."

"Yes, I've read it, and it's a guesstimate. It says the potential of the attacker was tall. I must insist you bring her in for questioning. You have local jurisdiction unless we decide to pull rank. I'd rather not since Althea has assured me your reputation speaks for itself, but I will if you continue to sit on your hands."

I balled my hands into fists under the table. "Fine. I'll do this your way." My cell buzzed again. "I need to get this." Withdrawing it from my pocket, I entered the hallway and closed the door. It was from Lily.

We've been watching the boat. Tom and Simone went fishing without bait, while the rest watched from shore. The women argued, but we only heard one side. You need to bring both women in for questioning. Meet me at the bookstore, and I'll explain.
XO L

Could I justify bringing in both women, and how did Lily know about the argument? But the bigger question is, how would I explain all this to the agents in my conference room? I hesitated. Should I return to the agents and fill them in or track down Peabody to let her know I needed her to be here during Susan Fisher's questioning?

The need to follow protocol won out, and I walked into the oversized room where Peabody and Mac sat at their desks.

She looked up. "What can we do to help?"

"Bring in Susan Fisher and Simone Holden. We need to question them. Check the marina first."

They pushed back their chairs. Mac said, "I'll let you know when we're on the way in."

I turned back. "Peabody, take Shepard. And Mac, you go with Jonesy. I'd like to see if either of the women talks to you on the way back. Nervous chatter."

"You got it, boss." Peabody was on her cell. "I'll call the others and have them meet us out back."

Mac nodded. "Is there anything more you can tell us?"

My face was grim. "The agents believe one

of them killed Todd Fisher, and until I can question them, they won't drop it."

"Didn't EL state it was likely a man due to the angle of the blow?"

I nodded. "Flores isn't listening to me or EL. Until I can prove to her these women aren't guilty and point to who it is, I'm in the hot seat to follow their direction." And it was a place I wanted to get out of as quickly as possible.

"Who do you like for the murder?"

"Felix Andrus. His prints came back. He faced charges of assault and battery, but the prosecution dropped the charges after the victim refused to testify."

"Why did they back out?"

I ran my hand over my jawline. "Felix and the others have connections to a powerful and vengeful family."

"I get you. No witness, no crime, and he walks."

"You got it. This time, if we can get something from the ladies, I can slowly tighten the noose and convince them talking is in everyone's best interest, including their own. Who knows when Felix or one of his partners in crime might turn on them? They won't be safe, not really."

"I'll radio in as soon as we're on our way back. If you need anything else while we're out, text."

"Head to the marina. Lily said Simone was on a boat, and Susan and the boys were watching them from the benches. You should hurry. I have a suspicion that since the first two seem to have failed in their attempt to retrieve the bag, the rest will try their luck at fishing for satchels."

He grinned. "You say satchels in the same breath as I'd say fishing for stripers."

"Yeah, buddy, you're a riot. Now take off before the agents decide I need to do something different."

I waited until the back door closed behind Mac and Peabody. My two trusted detectives wouldn't let me down. Instead of returning to the conference room, I closed the door to my office. I needed details that only Lily could provide.

When I heard her say hello, I briefly closed my eyes and allowed her voice to soothe my jangling nerves—or what was left of them. I hated having to keep her in the dark about this investigation, and whatever she could tell me, I wouldn't be able to reciprocate.

"Hi, Lily. Are you and Nikki okay?"

"I'm going to guess we're better than you. By the sound of your voice, you've been through the wringer since I saw you a couple of hours ago."

"You have no idea. I'm going out on a limb here and will say you know things about our suspects?"

She paused. "You won't be able to answer questions, will you?"

"I wish, but I can't. I hate asking you what you've discovered, but I need your help. I've come to rely on your keen observations."

"Ah, thank you. In that case, I'll tell you everything we've learned."

"Good, I'm listening."

She explained they waited on the beach to see who would show up for the rental of Red's boat even though Tom rented it. I was surprised to hear that it was Tom and Simone. I thought it might be one of the others with him.

"As you can guess, they didn't find anything, but their conversation was enlightening."

A stab of fear gouged my heart. "Please don't tell me you stowed away."

"No, we were on the beach and watched them with binoculars, but I cast a listening spell that went as far as they did."

Relief rushed over me when I realized she had played this very safe for a change and not gotten too close to a suspected murderer.

"Nikki could watch the group of onlookers from our spot on the beach, and we were listening in on the conversation between Simone and Tom. At first, they were antagonistic, but when he pulled the kid's backpack from the water, he softened up. She's the tough one of the pair."

"That's an interesting observation. Did you learn anything else?"

"They want to get out of the life they're in, but it's probably too late, and they're in too deep until everything's resolved. Before you ask, that's how vague they were."

"Do you have a hypothesis?" I trusted Lily's instincts like I trusted my own.

"They're involved in the counterfeit scheme, and the stress has worn on them. Remember, this couple moves around every year, so they've made a series of poor decisions regarding their life and want a fresh start. It's like buyer's remorse has set in or something. You know, after you make a large purchase and realize it probably wasn't the best financial decision."

I knew what she meant. "They'll get a fresh start if this case continues to unravel with how it's going." I realized I had spoken without censoring my thoughts.

"Gage, does that mean Tom and Simone are the bad guys?"

"Lily, from what we've seen so far, they're all treading that fine line between right and wrong."

"I know."

I pressed my fingers over my eyes to reduce the lingering headache. "What happened when Tom and Simone brought the boat in?"

"While they were still on the water, Simone called Susan after Tom decided they were done looking. Susan wasn't happy the tracking device wasn't pinging."

"Imagine that." I was pleased that EL had turned it off. Not that it would have pinged from our evidence locker. There was a range of efficacy.

"Anyway, during the conversation, Susan was pretty upset. Simone told her to take the boat out and find the bag herself."

"Did Susan take the locator mechanism, too?"

"Yeah, about that. Once we knew the exchange was happening, we packed it in and left the beach. Simone and Tom are still planning on coming to the bookstore this afternoon, and I didn't want Mimi to be there alone. It's another opportunity to excavate the truth."

I finger-combed my hair and tugged at the collar of my shirt. Lily was putting herself in the direct line of fire by engaging anyone from this group. As far as I was concerned, it didn't matter that agents had infiltrated them. There was no way they'd blow their cover for Lily and Nikki. "I'll head to the bookstore as soon as I'm done here."

"Gage, try not to worry about us. Nikki said she'll stay at the bookstore until I'm ready to leave."

That gave me a small comfort. "I'm going to let Mac and Peabody know Simone will be at your store, and you say Susan is taking the boat out?" I hoped a detective got to her first. The sooner we clarified her alibi for the morning Todd was killed, the better.

"Are you saying you need to bring Simone in for questioning?"

I heard the curiosity pique in her voice.

"I'm not confirming or denying anything. Just let me know when she leaves and double-check your protection spell."

"Try not to worry. I'm wearing my necklace, so it'll tell me if there's danger, and the charms around the shop are strong."

"That's reassuring." I exhaled, but still, the worry wouldn't leave me.

"Gage, are you alone?"

"Yes, why?"

"Remember how EL hung out when you left with Sharon and Mac?"

I felt a rush of adrenaline and wasn't sure I'd like what I was about to hear. "Did something happen?"

"Yes, and no. He was hinting around about Nikki's kitchen ability and asked her to bake a cake for Sharon's birthday next month."

"That hardly sounds like a reason for concern." Lily wasn't one to let something minor unsettle her.

"He told us, Nikki and me, that he's a witch. We didn't confirm or deny our status. I asked my aunt, and she said he didn't belong to our coven. Do you know what his status is, and if he is a real, live cauldron-stirring witch? Why didn't anyone know about him?"

I slumped in my chair. "I don't know what you're talking about. As far as I know, EL is a brainiac in science and an excellent doctor, but he has a passion for police work, so he moved into the medical examiner's role."

"Exactly, so why would a man be so smart, who we've discovered is a witch, live in a small town, and work with a small police force that, until the last couple of years, maintained order in a bucolic little place."

"Sweetheart, I can't answer that question today. Maybe we can table it until this current investigation is complete?" My thoughts raced. How could I confront EL and protect all the witches I care about?

"You're right."

She sounded like she was just handed a deflated balloon. "I just got back to the store, but before I go inside, what about Chuck Yancy?"

"What about him?" I knew where this conversation was going to go.

"You asked him about fake bills, and he passed one to William. How could he not know it was fake, or do you think it was deliberate to get the police department's attention?"

I hadn't thought of that angle. "Honestly, I haven't given his involvement a lot of thought. But if it makes you feel better, I checked him out, and his reputation in the banking industry is solid. He worked his way up from a teller in various institutions until he got this job. I can't find a blemish on his resume."

Lily said, "Gage, don't you think that in itself could be a red flag or at least a yellow one?"

Chapter 19
Lily

Aunt Mimi closed the bookstore door, and with a quick magic spell, I was dressed in a cute skirt and top. Nikki also changed our beach wear to look like a shopgirl. All that was left was for Simone and Tom to walk in. I made another circle around the store, my fingers running over the covers of books, selecting titles I thought she might find captivating.

"Lily, why are you going to all the trouble of selecting books? Don't you think Tom and

Simone are coming in more to gain information than she wants reading material?"

I glanced at Nikki with a smile. "I'm going to hold up my end of the charade." I picked up a book and turned it over to read the jacket. "Nikki, is it possible the group thinks Todd was a snitch to the feds and they killed him before he could reveal critical information that would bring them down?"

"Anything's possible, but if that's the case and he was working for the government, does that mean Susan would have been as well? As a married couple, they would share information and maybe even similar points of view." Her eyes widened. "Do you think Susan could be in danger?"

"No. It's obvious she's working with them, unless she's a great actress. If he told her he was planning on turning in his gang members that could have been his undoing and one of them decided to eliminate the threat."

"Unless she didn't know what they're capable of doing." Nikki shivered and ran a hand over her arm. "That sounds sinister. Gangs in Pembroke Cove."

I placed the book down and walked behind the counter. "I don't know how else to think of the group." I sat on the stool and propped my chin in my hand. "How does Chuck Yancy fit into all of this?"

Nikki said, "Pull him up on the internet. Let's do some digging." She settled into a wing-back chair at the front of the store. "I'm going to keep an eye open in case you need to shut down your screen."

Milo trotted in from the back and hopped onto the counter. "Hello, my dear witch." His gaze traveled over my arms. "What did you learn at the beach? Other than that, you should have worn more sunscreen; your arms will need lotion tonight. We can stop at Mimi's before going home. She has just the potion to get rid of the pink."

"No need to worry about my sunburn. This case is what we need to focus on." I tapped the screen. "We're checking up on the new vice president of the bank. He passed William a counterfeit bill after Gage interviewed him."

He grumbled, "Do you think he could be a part of this or an innocent bystander like William?"

"I'm not sure. Until he came to town, no one had ever heard of him. I find it very interesting that he arrived mere weeks before summer, and for the first time that I'm aware of, we have counterfeit money in town."

"Good point." He pawed the screen. "What are you waiting for? Get searching!"

I wanted to remind Milo that he had interrupted me, but I didn't. "I'm starting with his bio on the bank's website. It should give things like his previous experience and education."

Nikki said, "Good idea. Milo, come sit with me, and you can help with street surveillance."

He paused in his face washing. "Are you asking for help so I won't bother my witch?"

She laughed. "Not at all. You can still swipe at her verbally from here. But with the two of us watching, we can be ready for anyone coming in either direction."

As if weighing his options, Milo hesitated and finally hopped down, trotted across the floor before jumping to Nikki's lap and then perched on the back of the chair. "I've got the right, and you take the left."

She reached behind her head and scratched his ears. "Thanks."

Watching them from the corner of my eye, I saw Milo's ears soften, and a purr of contentment escaped his little body.

I zeroed in on Chuck's bio. The font was so small that I had to enlarge the screen with a little magic. "Charles Yancy, VP of our little bank. He went to the University of Pittsburgh and studied finance. He's risen up the corporate ladder quickly, but nothing on here is a red flag. He's just a go-getter."

"There's nothing wrong with that."

"Nik, I'm going to do a wide search to see if anything irregular happened in any of the locations where he worked."

She glanced my way. "Like a funny money breakout."

I nodded and stayed focused on the screen. While I worked, I said, "The bank wouldn't have hired him if he had a criminal record. But if he was good at deflecting and casting suspicion on another person in the bank, he could be dirty and still get away clean."

I scanned the search results, but nothing stood out as hinky. "I've got nothing." I closed the laptop and slumped on the stool. "Maybe he's like William, innocent in all this. But I want to ask him where he got the bill from."

Nikki sat up. "You might get your chance. He's headed in this direction."

I jumped up and hurried to get a better view of the street. Sure enough, Chuck was crossing the town green, a straight line from the bank to my door.

He pushed open the door and flashed a wide smile at Nikki and me. "Afternoon, ladies."

"Good afternoon, Chuck. It's a lovely day out."

"It sure is. Nothing like Maine in the summer, is there?" He made a beeline for the best-seller table. "My boxes haven't arrived yet. From what I've been told, they got lost in transit. Sadly, I'm out of reading materials."

I smiled at him and walked closer to the table. "Is this the first time you've been in my store?"

"It is. I'm just getting to know the shop owners in town. So far, I've eaten at the Copper Kettle, Tucker's Hardware has been immensely helpful, and the Sweet Spot has the best cinnamon buns I've tasted."

"They're my favorite, too." Since he brought up William's bakery, I thought it was the perfect opening to discuss the money. "Did you know someone paid William a phony one-hundred-dollar bill?" I watched Nikki wince at my direct approach.

"That's awful. He needs to report it to Gage. Have you heard of any others?"

I shook my head and found it interesting that he mentioned Gage specifically. "No, and I don't accept large bills."

He frowned. "You don't. That's all I have on me."

I glanced at the floor, attempting to appear like I wasn't about to pounce, and casually said, "Did you use a large bill at the Sweet Spot?"

Color flushed his face. His tone went from pleasant to hostile. "Are you accusing me of passing bad bills?"

"Not at all, merely asking a simple question." I gave him my sweet and innocent smile, which I had to practice years ago when I started working in the bookstore to ease a nasty customer into being nicer or at least tolerable.

"I'm sorry, Lily. Forgive me. I enjoy living here. It already feels like home. For someone to think that I would deliberately pass money that isn't real is a gut punch." He rubbed his midsection as if for emphasis. He withdrew his wallet. "Here, I've got a couple more. Look at them, and you'll see." He handed me the bills.

That was not the way a guilty man acted. Nikki said, "More customers are coming." She took the bills from me and said, "I've got this." She went behind the counter and placed them on it.

I turned and smiled as Tom and Simone entered. I glanced at the clock, and it was four on the dot. "Welcome to the Cozy Nook. I'm glad you got here before I closed."

Simone smiled, and Tom nodded to Chuck.

She said, "I know we've arrived at closing time, but the day's been hectic. Were you able to select a few titles for me?" Her gaze traveled the room. "Tom, I'm going to need time to browse. This store is charming."

He said, "Would you mind if I sat? My wife will be here until you kick us out."

I gestured to the wing-back chair that Milo was sitting on. "Relax. Can I get you a coffee or tea, perhaps?" I remember Simone's crack about food and beverages in town and winced. I didn't need to defend my mother's tea blends to him or anyone.

"No, thanks." He rested his ankle over the opposite knee. "I'm used to waiting."

Nikki cleared her throat and nodded at the counter. The bills were fake.

"Chuck. Any chance I could see you in the other room?"

He took a step back. "Don't tell me."

I didn't want to, not in front of the Holdens. With a sweeping motion, I gestured to the back room. "Please."

Simone stopped perusing the shelf in front of her. We had captured her attention. I didn't miss the arched brow as she looked at Tom.

"Fine. But I'm innocent of any wrongdoing."

I needed to get him away from the Holdens before he said something that would tip them off that the local cops were on to them.

He stalked into the room, and I closed the door, touching my amulet. It was cool as a cucumber. I cast a quick silencing spell so the customers couldn't overhear our conversation.

"Chuck, where did you get the money?"

"At the bank. I cashed a check. Carrying big bills keeps me mindful of my spending. If I have twenties and below, they're like water through my fingers. This way, I think twice about breaking a large bill. I've been doing it for years."

"Any idea how the money would have gotten into the bank's drawers with no one catching on?"

He shook his head. "Everyone should scan them." Muttering to himself, "This will be disastrous."

I placed my hand on his arm. "You need to call the bank and have all bills scanned before business tomorrow."

"There's nothing I can do today. The bank's closed. But the morning's a different story."

I nodded. "I'll call Gage, and he'll come over. You can tell him what's happened and what your plan is."

He sank to a chair at the small table. "Can I wait here?"

"Yes." I dropped the spell from the door

and said, "Help yourself to coffee. I'll be out front waiting on my customers." My hand paused on the knob. "Chuck, the couple out front. Have you seen them in the bank in the last week or two?"

His frown lines deepened. "Not that I recall. Should I have?"

"No, just curious." As I walked out, Tom glanced up as Simone flipped through a book.

"Nikki, thanks for covering me. I need to step outside for a minute."

"Go ahead, I've got this."

I closed the door and glanced around to make sure no one was within hearing distance. I dialed.

"Erikson."

I guessed he hadn't looked at the screen to know who it was. "It's me. I need you to get over to the bookstore. Chuck Yancy is here, and he was going to pay with, you know what. And the Holdens are here. I'm sure they're the killers. I'm going to stall."

"What? Never mind. Don't do anything

except talk books. Please wait for me before you unearth information. I'll be there as fast as I can."

"Bring the team and have some come through the back. Chuck is in the storage room, and I have a funny feeling things are about to get very interesting."

I hung up, and my heart sank to my stomach. Susan and the three stooges were coming across the grass. As they reached the sidewalk, I plastered a welcoming smile on my face. "Hello, welcome to the Cozy Nook Bookstore."

Susan said, "I'm glad you're still open."

My fingers itched to let Gage know the rest of the group had joined the party. "Please come in. We're staying open a bit later today but closing in twenty minutes." I felt the warmth of my amulet through my blouse. That was never a good thing.

Susan, Felix, Eddie, and Wilbur walked in single file and dispersed in different directions. They ignored Tom and Simone. I knew they were all acquainted, and coming together didn't bode well for them. However, it was the perfect opportunity to ask lots of questions.

Milo jumped from the back of the chair and wound his body between my legs. "Be careful, Lily. I'm not sure who does what, but they're all up to no good."

I scooped him up and kissed the top of his gray head. "Why don't you sit on the counter to avoid getting stepped on?"

Nikki scanned the room as if mentally placing them all. Her cell rang. "It's Steve."

I didn't want him to come to the store and get in the middle of this. As a non-magical, he had little protection if it was two witches and a familiar against six non-magicals, and who knew if they had weapons? Seven if I counted Chuck.

"Ask Steve to meet us at my place for dinner around six?" I hoped she'd catch my line of thinking.

"Hello there, handsome," she drifted to the back of the store, I assumed for privacy.

I stood behind the counter, which gave me

the best vantage point to keep an eye on everyone. The only downside was that Chuck was behind me.

Milo said, "I've got eyes on the VP."

I didn't acknowledge him, but he knew. This wasn't our first time watching customers in the shop.

"Did you all enjoy your day in town?" I decided that asking a general question was the best way to gauge their response.

Susan said, "Uneventful. We went fishing for a while but didn't catch anything."

"I heard nothing was biting today." I straightened Simone's stack of books.

Susan looked sharply at Simone, who lifted her shoulder opposite from me as if I couldn't see her.

Wilbur leaned against the counter like a bar, pulling a small handgun from behind his back to make sure I saw it. "Do you fish often?"

"Occasionally. My friends and fiancé were out on Sunday. We had to cut the day short because of a police matter."

"Really? I've heard you and the cops in town are pretty tight."

I shifted from one foot to the other. "I'm engaged to Detective Erikson. We're going to be married in September." Why was I babbling? I needed to use Gage's silent method if I was going to get anywhere with these people.

"We saw you standing over Todd Fisher." He flicked his gun in Felix and Eddie's direction. "You know, from the park."

I licked my lips. "I remember."

"Which one of us do you think whacked him with that rock?" He took a step closer, and Milo grumbled deep in his throat. I ran my hand down his back, hoping he'd give me more time to uncover the truth.

Eddie pulled out a gun and held it at his side. "It was an accident. The rock was supposed to miss him."

I half turned to look Eddie in the eyes. "Did you throw it?" I heard a pistol cock, and my gut twisted. I could disarm one, but not multiple guns. I really needed to read my book to make my spells more broad-based.

"I told you to read it." Milo brushed his body against my arm.

Tom brandished a gun in the air. "Everyone just needs to settle down, and no one will get hurt."

Chapter 20
Lily

What was taking Gage so long? Now, everyone had a gun either pointed at someone or me. How the heck had that happened?

"Excuse me, why's everyone yelling?" Nikki came around the corner of an aisle, and her words died.

"We seem to have a situation." I paused before I said "situation" because I was unsure what to call it.

"I see." She moved slowly until she stood next to me.

I didn't know a spell that could stop a bullet or create a shield to withstand one.

Milo's claws pressed into my hand. "Lily, ask the nervous guy who killed the vic."

I wanted to remind him we were in a precarious situation, but I had learned to trust my familiar. "Eddie, since you're saying it was an accident, why don't you tell me what happened? I'm sure once you do, the police will understand."

He snorted. "They never do. Accidents are always a crime. But since we're leaving town when we walk outta here, I guess there's no harm. We're like the wind."

Susan said, "Everyone needs to shut up. A bookstore clerk can't do anything even if she's marrying a cop. He's not here."

"Exactly my point." He waved the gun at Susan and Simone. "Ladies, join us on this side of the store."

They did as he asked, and moments later, Nikki and I had six people standing before us, holding weapons.

Simone nudged Susan's arm. "Didn't expect this today, did you?"

Susan rolled her eyes. "The only luck we've had since we got here was bad."

Eddie said, "Except for the five hundred bucks we got from the bank, right, Sophia?"

Susan growled, "Shut up, Eddie, before you spill all the deets."

Neither woman responded to the different name directly, but it didn't take long to realize that was an important clue Gage had withheld from me.

I pushed my shoulders back and down. "Who threw the rock that killed Todd, if that's his real name?"

Wilbur grinned. "You're a tough lady, asking questions. But since you've asked, I'll tell ya."

Eddie's tone was threatening. "Back off, Wilbur."

"Eh, what's she gonna do? We'll tell her what happened and be a ghost." He moved to stand with the others. "Felix threw the rock.

He's never had a decent aim. In hindsight, Sophia should have tossed it. She played ball in high school."

Simone glanced at Tom. "Okay, that's enough confession time. Let's hit the road."

Nikki grabbed my hand. "Not so fast. Susan, didn't Eddie say you got money from the bank? How did you pull off exchanging counterfeit for the real thing?"

Her eyes widened briefly, and she tugged on her ear. "These women are far from harmless. What else do they know about?"

Following Nikki's question, I stepped around the counter, between the gun-toting criminals and her. Milo hissed at me. A cold shiver of fear raced down my spine.

"A friend of mine was paid with a counterfeit bill. Coincidently, it was after you rolled into town."

"I'll give you one thing, Lily. You're smarter than I originally thought," Simone sneered. "Come on, we should take off. We've been here too long already."

"What about the car everyone said dropped Todd? Surveillance cameras showed he stumbled up the walk."

Wilbur shook his head. "Stupid lie. No one should have ever mentioned a vehicle that didn't exist. Todd was going to talk to the cops. We had to stop him."

Simone tapped her foot on the floor. She had to be Sophia. She was itching to get away. "Susan?"

She snapped her fingers. "Do I have to spell it out? You go to the bank and exchange big bills for smaller ones. It makes sense since the stores here have signs saying *No Big Bills*. We pass off the bills and get real money. It happens more often than you realize."

"As far as Todd is concerned, I'll miss him, he was a decent husband." She leveled her gun at me. "Now that you know how we work, maybe it's time we say goodbye. Permanently."

My heart thudded in my chest, and my mouth went dry. Was she going to shoot me right here in front of Milo and Nikki? *Oh, Gage. I pushed too hard, again.*

Simone placed her hand on Susan's arm. "She's not worth it." Nodding to the door, she said, "Felix, you, Eddie, and Wilbur take off. We'll bring Susan with us and meet you in Portland."

Tom nodded. "Go."

There was no way I was letting them leave. Even if Gage hadn't arrived, he'd be here soon and could make the arrests. I stared at the lock on the door, and it clicked.

Nikki sucked in a breath. We were trapped with very unsavory characters.

Eddie grabbed the knob, but the door wouldn't budge. "Hey, lady, unlock this door."

I crossed my arms over my chest. "It's not locked."

"Smash a window and open it from the other side." Susan strode over and, using the butt of her gun, hit the pane of glass, but it bounced back.

Nikki's eyes widened. "When did you...?"

"Quiet." Simone barked. She faced me, pointing her gun at the floor. "Look, I'm doing my best to keep Susan from scratching the itch on her index finger. Cut us some slack and unlock the door. We'll be gone, and you don't need to feel bad for letting us go." She tipped her head and stared at me.

My amulet cooled. Simone wasn't going to hurt me. "I told you it's not locked. You can leave whenever you want." I imagined blowing a flame to the door handle, and from where I stood, I thought it had a slight glow of heat.

Tom flicked the gun from me to the door. "Prove it."

"I'm not about to walk in front of you while you're pointing that at me." I had to stall for time. Gage would come through the back, and they'd have a clear shot at him. I glanced over my shoulder. Chuck wasn't sitting at the table. Where was he?

Even though my statement challenged him,

my amulet was cool against my skin. This was very interesting. It was like it was helping me separate the good guys from the bad.

Felix and Wilbur each took a menacing step toward me.

Nikki said, "Try it again."

Eddie cried out in pain as he turned the knob. "My hand." He held it up, as blisters formed.

Simone said, "This has gone far enough. I'm not sure why you think detaining us will help you, but do yourself a favor and open the door." Her face was obscured as she mouthed, "*Please.*"

What kind of criminal is polite? Was Simone in law enforcement? Something in my peripheral vision drew my attention. Sharon Peabody was creeping along the front of Twisted Scissors Hair Salon. Backup had arrived.

Chuck walked around one of the bookshelves. "Sophia. This has gone on long enough. Open the door. We're leaving." He jabbed a finger in my direction. "You're getting out of this unscathed because of your gullibility to think I wouldn't know the difference between real and fake money. I've worked in banking for a long time and been around the production of money even longer." He tapped his brow. "It's been nice meeting you, Lily. You've got a great store. Too bad we didn't have time to shop."

I didn't appreciate his sarcastic tone and assumption he could just walk out of here? Ha.

Susan walked over to Chuck and slipped her arm around his waist. The implication hit me: Susan was Sophia, and Sophia was at the center of this case.

"Hold on. For my curiosity, can you clear something up for me, Chuck?"

He glanced at his watch. "I can spare you one minute."

"Todd was a part of your group. Someone got ticked off because he dropped a satchel full of counterfeit money in the ocean, and several of you have spent the last few days trying to retrieve it."

A gleam came into his eye. "I underestimated you. How do you know about the money in the bag?"

I pointed to Nikki and gave her a small smile. "We pulled it from the water before Todd was killed."

"Great." Chuck threw up his hands. "That chicken decided to turn his back on his wife and friends and confess everything. We were all packed and ready to leave town until he decided to tell the local PD about the waterlogged bag. The guys tried to convince him otherwise. We didn't know Felix would get lucky and take care of the weak link. We were hoping to deter Todd, not kill him." He shrugged. "Sometimes, things have a way of going in a different direction. After he died, Sophia discovered information he'd written down, the bag had a GPS tracking device. Instead of leaving, we tried to find it. You know, waste not and all."

"Besides, there's no sense polluting the ocean." Susan, who was really Sophia, said. "Now, open the door, or that little cat will have used up his ninth life." She waved her gun in Milo's direction.

That was all it took for me to stop waiting and act. I took one step to my left and put my body between Milo and the gun. The only spell that came to mind was the banishing spell. Would it work here? In a clear, calm voice, I said, "I bend these guns that threaten me, making them useless against thee. As for this, I decree, so it shall be." Before my eyes, the barrels of the guns bent downward like melted candles sitting in the August sun. *Where did that come from?*

Sophia pulled the trigger on her gun. "What's happening?"

Chuck blinked rapidly. "This has to be my imagination. Guns don't melt."

The front door burst open, and Officer Shepard strode through it. "Hands up.

Undo the last spell I used to protect me. So it shall be.

Jonesy was right behind him, followed by Mac. Gage and Sharon burst in from the back room, guns drawn.

Gage shouted. "Everyone freeze!" He glanced at me. "Are you okay?"

I tipped my head and smiled. "Yes. Arrest all of them, including Chuck. He appears to be a leader, along with Susan, whose real name is Sophia."

He shook his head and laughed while he slapped cuffs on Chuck. Sharon did the same for Susan aka Sophia.

Two women stepped into the store and looked around.

"I'm sorry, the store is closed." One woman looked vaguely familiar, with penetrating dark eyes and black hair. Then it hit me. "Althea Peters?"

"Agent Peters, but yes. This is my partner, Agent Flores." She nodded. "I see my cousin's characterization of you was spot on."

"I'll take that as a compliment."

The other agent frowned. "Can you tell us what happened here?"

"Well, it's a long story, but the short version is that Felix killed Todd, and Susan is Sophia. I'm not sure how that's relevant since I don't have a last name. Chuck, the bank VP, seems to be involved with the counterfeit group. Eddie and Wilbur have been somewhat menacing, and everyone is holding me, Nikki, and Milo at gunpoint. As a final point, they all know about the satchel in the ocean." I gestured to everyone who was now in handcuffs. "I present to you the gang." For extra emphasis, I used air quotes around *gang*.

"How did you come by this information?" Agent Flores glared at Gage. "Did you break confidentiality?"

He held onto Chuck's upper arm. "I gave my word and kept it. If you need proof, ask Agent Peters' cousin, Chief Peters, formerly Special Agent Peters. He'll vouch for my integrity and Lily's uncanny ability to solve a crime."

Her brow arched. "Really?"

"Gage, how about I explain my love of puzzles to Agents Flores and Peters tomorrow night? For right now, you have criminals to process."

He gave me a wink. "You heard the lady. Let's take our prisoners and vacate her store."

Shepard had paired a suspect with an officer, except for Althea. I was sure he used a dose of magic for an added measure of security.

Althea waited until everyone had gone outside. "Lily, I want to thank you and say that Nola Flores is a good agent. She was more concerned for your safety than Gage's potential breach of confidentiality."

"Thank you for telling me that. I don't want Gage to be in trouble for my actions, and he would never break his word."

"Don't give it another thought, and if that dinner offer still stands for tomorrow night, mind if I bring a couple of guests with me?"

"The more, the merrier." On impulse, I hugged her. She was so like Dax, my brother from another mother.

The next afternoon, Nikki and I set up for the party. She placed a cooler of ice on a small table. "Yesterday was crazy."

"I know. Who would have thought all the suspects in the forgery and murder of Todd Fisher would end up in my bookstore at the same time?"

She crossed her arms and leaned against the railing. "How did you know to do the spell about the guns? Making them all useless."

I shrugged. "I didn't. I've meant to read my book of magic and see if I can cast multiple spells simultaneously, but I've never found the time. So, yesterday, the only spell that sprang to mind was the banishing spell, which didn't apply. So, I focused on making the guns not work. Then, just as the officers were walking in the door, I undid the spell, and no one was the wiser."

"You're amazing. Most witches don't have to use magic to save lives or even change them. We use it to make our day jobs easier, clean our homes, and, you know, do little stuff that, in the grand scheme, is meaningless. It was generations ago when magic saved our ancestors from harm."

"Aunt Mimi changes lives with her healing."

Nikki nodded. "She does, but you've had to think on your feet and become creative in the spur of the moment. No other witch I know does that unless they're up to no good."

"What do you think it means?"

She opened her mouth to say something when the slamming car doors reached us. "We'll talk about it another time."

"We can go inside and talk if it's important."

With a shake of her head, she smiled. "No. Tonight is a celebration. We should have fun."

Sharon and EL came up the stairs first, and he carried a bowl of greens. "Our contribution."

Nola Flores was behind them and held out her hand to shake mine. "Thank you for inviting me. Althea's waiting for a couple of people in the driveway." She glanced over her shoulder. "There they are now."

Dax ran up the stairs and opened his arms. I ran across the deck and threw myself into them. "You came! I left you a message, but you didn't return my call."

He kissed my cheek. "Are you kidding? I had to come and hear about your latest case, and of course, the chance to see my cousin was icing on the cake." He peered over my shoulder. "Any chance Nikki brought dessert?"

For his ears only I asked, "Can I fly a broom?"

He laughed. "We'll catch up later. I need to make the rounds now."

Althea laughed as she drew closer to the house, and my mouth gaped open. What were they doing here?

"Lily, I'd like to introduce you to two of our exceptional agents, Simone and Tom Holden."

"Welcome?" I did a double take. "You're agents?" Then I remembered the fleeting sensation of my amulet cooling when Simone talked to me yesterday.

She took my hand. "I'm sorry, Lily, but we've been undercover for a while, and now that Sophia's been arrested, the rest of the forgery ring collapsed like dominoes. All thanks to you. When Althea invited us tonight, I wasn't sure if we should come, but Tom and I wanted to thank you for everything you did."

"I'm glad you came, and you might have heard I love a good puzzle. Please enjoy yourselves."

Althea gave me a quick hug. "You're exactly like Dax said, and you must tell me about the spell you used to eavesdrop on the boat conversation. Gage shared that minor detail with me. It was ingenious and powerful."

I nodded. "Sure, we can talk."

Milo slunk out of the kitchen door, and I scooped him up.

He grumbled, "Before the party begins, I wanted to thank you." He butted his head against my chin. "I know what you did at the store. Putting yourself between me and that woman."

"You would have done it for me." I kissed the top of his soft fur.

"Can I ask a favor?"

I was glad he changed the subject. The idea of losing him was more than I could bear tonight. I wanted to have fun and relax. "If I can."

"Will you read your book of magic and see if you can find a spell to help that big lug, Brutus, communicate with—or at least be able to understand me? Detective Cutie is getting better, but that...beast, that's moving into our home —" he patted my cheek. "You gotta help me."

Before I could answer, he jumped down. "I'll try," I called after him.

He trotted down the steps as Gage was

coming up. He slipped his arm around my waist and kissed my cheek.

Milo stopped in front of Brutus and swished his tail several times, and the dog followed him across the backyard. I sighed. Wasn't that communication?

Gage asked, "What are you thinking?"

"This is our chosen family. Not that we don't love our other family, but these people are here because we've formed strong, unbreakable bonds."

He held me close. "We're lucky." Glancing my way, he said, "Did you do something fun today?"

"Maybe."

"Oh?" I loved how his face lit up when he knew I was up to something.

"Nikki and I decided when we go shopping at Grant's Gowns, we're making it a girls' day."

Wrapping his arms around me, Gage held me close. "Do you think there's a chance our wedding will go off like an average couple?"

I laughed. "Maybe I should gaze into a cup of tea leaves."

He looked me in the eye and laughed, "No. The last time you tried to read tea leaves, you discovered a murder." With a kiss on my forehead, he said, "We're getting married. What could go wrong?"

Please leave a review now!
Are you ready to read more from the Lily and the gang in Pembroke?
Keep reading for a sneak peek at
Weddings & Wands
A Book Store Cozy Mystery Series
Order Now
Or
Shop at Lucinda Race

I hope you want to keep up with my crazy antics of writing, gardening, cooking, and life with the pups.

Lucinda

Not ready to stop reading yet? If you sign up for my newsletter at www.lucindarace.com/newsletter, you will receive a novella for Cookies & Capers, the introduction of when Lily met Milo, as my thank-you gift for choosing to get my newsletter.

Weddings and Wands

Welcome to Pembroke Cove, where witches and murders are multiplying...

In less than a week, wedding bells will ring for Gage Erikson—a.k.a. Detective Cutie—and bookstore owner and witch Lily Michaels. Lily's to-do list is already a mile long. Adding "solve a murder" wasn't part of the plan. But they have little choice when Lily discovers a dead Elemental witch across the street, revealing a grudge that threatens to upend not just their big day, but the entire Pembroke Cove coven.

Long ago, the Elementals had grown jealous of the power wielded by the witches in the Pembroke Cove coven, vowing to return and take their rightful place within the coven council...triggered by a leadership change. Meanwhile, Lily learns her wedding will be the catalyst and wishes she'd actually read the entire witch's handbook.

Gage is determined to keep his puzzle-loving fiancé out of the case this time—no murder board. No sleuthing. The only thing he wants to discuss with her is their wedding. However, not even the elements of earth, wind, water, or fire will stop Lily's investigation. But will they stop the wedding? It will take all of Lily and Gage's witchy friends, family, and Lily's familiar—the talking cat, Milo—to solve a murder and pull off the long-awaited wedding. It's a good thing Lily and Gage have the most potent magic in the universe on their side— love.

* * *

Visit Pembroke Cove in this charming supernatural tale where bookshops meet broomsticks and Lily and Gage will need more than magical abilities to make it to "I do."

**Weddings & Wands
A Book Store Cozy Mystery Series
Order Now**

Weddings and Wands

Welcome to Pembroke Cove, where witches and murders are multiplying...

In less than a week, wedding bells will ring for Gage Erikson—a.k.a. Detective Cutie—and bookstore owner and witch Lily Michaels. Lily's to-do list is already a mile long. Adding "solve a murder" wasn't part of the plan. But they have little choice when Lily discovers a dead Elemental witch across the street, revealing a grudge that threatens to upend not just their big day, but the entire Pembroke Cove coven.

Long ago, the Elementals had grown jealous of the power wielded by the witches in the Pembroke Cove coven, vowing to return and take their rightful place within the coven council...triggered by a leadership change. Meanwhile, Lily learns her wedding will be the catalyst and wishes she'd actually read the entire witch's handbook.

Gage is determined to keep his puzzle-loving fiancé out of the case this time—no murder board. No sleuthing. The only thing he wants to discuss with her is their wedding. However, not even the elements of earth, wind, water, or fire will stop Lily's investigation. But will they stop the wedding? It will take all of Lily and Gage's witchy friends, family, and Lily's familiar—the talking cat, Milo—to solve a murder and pull off the long-awaited wedding. It's a good thing Lily and Gage have the most potent magic in the universe on their side—love.

* * *

Visit Pembroke Cove in this charming supernatural tale where bookshops meet broomsticks and Lily and Gage will need more than magical abilities to make it to "I do."

Order Now

A Free Story for You

Have you enjoyed Fishing & Forgery? Not ready to stop reading yet? If you sign up for my newsletter at www.lucindarace.com/newsletter, you will receive Cookies & Capers, which is the start of Lily and Milo's adventure, as my thank-you gift for choosing to get my newsletter.

Cookies & Capers

I stood in front of the old wood and glass door as I pocketed the keys to the Cozy Nook

Bookshop. Aunt Mimi had signed her bookstore over to me. She said it felt like giving me her baby. But I loved the shop as much as my aunt did. We had worked together for the last twelve years. After attending the University of Maine, I had a degree in history and education. I had always wanted to be a teacher, but jobs were scarce and after substituting for a few years, I moved back to my hometown of Pembroke, Maine, and Aunt Mimi hired me as soon as I unpacked my suitcase.

Spending time with my aunt, learning the business, had been the best experience. I offered to buy the shop when she wanted to retire, but she wouldn't hear of it. As long as she had free books for life, and her long-term boyfriend Nate, she said it was a fair deal. From my point of view, I had built-in backup for years to come.

Now that I was the bookshop owner, Aunt Mimi was no longer coming in every day which meant her cat, Phoenix, wasn't either and the space felt empty without a kitty lying in the window or skulking about as kitties do. I was off to the Pembroke Animal Palace to see if I could find a match.

It was a short walk in the bright noonday sun. The spring air from the ocean carried a tang of salt, but the breeze was refreshing. I waved to one of my best friends, Gage Erikson, as he drove past in his police-issued sedan. My heart fluttered in my chest.

He was a detective on the force. Not that we had much crime in our small seaside town. But one of these days I was going to get brave and tell him I had been carrying a torch for him since we were in ninth grade. What's the worst thing that could happen? We'd still be best friends, right?

Cookies & Capers is only available by signing up for my newsletter – sign up for it here at www.lucindarace.com/newsletter

Love to Read?

**All ebooks and paperback copies can
be ordered from my website at:
Shop at Lucinda Race**

Cozy Mystery Books

A Bookstore Cozy Mystery Series
Books & Bribes
*It was an ordinary day until the book of
Practical Magic conked Lily on the head
causing her to see stars. And then she discovered
her cat, Milo, could talk.*

what's up with the coven's council? Can Lily unravel this new mystery before she says, I do.

Ghostly Gowns Series
A Paranormal Ghost Cozy Mystery Series

Ghost and Gowns June 2025
Buttons & Burglary July 2025
Ribbons & Robbery August 2025

Witches of Robins Pointe
A Paranormal Cozy Mystery Series

Inherited Magic & Murder January 2026
Touch of Magic February 2026
Waiting for Magic March 2026

Cowboys of River Junction

Second Chances in Montana

Twenty years later, Renee and Hank are back where they fell in love, but reality is like a spring frost, and is a long-distance relationship their only option for their second chance?

Stars Over Montana
The cowboy broke her heart, but he never stopped loving her. Now, she's back ready to run her grandfather's ranch...

Hiding in Montana
Can love flourish while danger lurks in the shadows?

Moonlight Over Montana
From the smoldering ash, she realizes he's all the family she and her daughter need.

Standalone Titles

Shamrocks are a Girl's Best Friend
Will a bit of Irish luck and a matchmaking uncle give Kelly and Tric a chance to find love?

The Matchmaker and The Marine
She vowed never to love again. His career in the Marines crushed his ability to love. Can undeniable chemistry and a leap of faith overcome their past?

<u>Sundaes on Sunday</u>
A widowed school teacher and the airline pilot

whose little girl is determined to bring her daddy and the lady from the ice cream shop together for a second chance at love.

Barrett

Has the last man standing finally met his match?

Marie

Career-focused city girl discovers small town charm can lead to love.

Price Family Romance Series

Breathe

Her dream come true may be the end of his...

Crush

The first time they met was fleeting; the second time restarted her heart.

<u>Blush</u>

He's always loved her but he left and now he's back...the question, does she still love him?

Vintage

He's an unexpected distraction, she gets his engine running...

Love to Read?

Where do you go to heal your heart? You make the journey home...
The Last First Kiss
When life handed Kate lemons, she baked.
Ready to Soar
Kate will fight for love, won't she?
Love in the Looking Glass
Will Ellie's first love be her last or will she become a ghost like her father?
Magic in the Rain
Dani's plan of hiding in plain sight may not have been the best idea.
After All These Years
Arielle Clark is a famous artist with a painful past. When her first love comes to town, ghosts from the past are resurrected. But can the embers of love still linger after all these years?

Social Media

Follow Me on Social Media

Like my Facebook page
Join Lucinda's Heart Racer's Reader Group on
Facebook
Twitter @lucindarace
Instagram @lucindaraceauthor
BookBub
Goodreads
Pinterest
YouTube

About the Author

Award-winning and best-selling author Lucinda Race is an avid fan of fiction. As a young girl, she spent hours reading cozy mystery and romance novels, getting lost in the fun and hope they represented. While her friends dreamed of becoming doctors and engineers, she dreamed of becoming an expert at crafting captivating novels.

As life twisted and turned, she wrote nonfiction but longed to return to her true passion. After developing the storylines for the McKenna Family Romance series and the Paranormal Cozy Nook Bookstore Series, she decided to start living her dream. Her fingers practically fly over computer keys. She weaves paranormal cozy mystery stories and romance with guaranteed happily ever afters.

Lucinda lives with her two little dogs, a miniature long-haired dachshund and a shitzu mix rescue, in the rolling hills of western Massachusetts. When she's not immersed in her fictional worlds, writing mystery, suspense, and romance novels she's reading everything she can get her hands on.